The Crown Of Success

Charlotte Maria Tucker

Edition : Culturea (Hérault, 34)
Contact : infos@culturea.fr
Print in Germany by Books on Demand
Design and layout : Derek Murphy
Layout : Reedsy (https://reedsy.com/)
ISBN : 9791041951406
Légal deposit : September 2023

THE CROWN OF SUCCESS

CHAPTER I

THE DAME'S DEPARTURE.

A MERRY life had Dame Desley and her four children led in their rural home. The sound of their cheerful voices, the patter of their little feet, the laugh, the shout, and the song, had been heard from morning till night. I will not stop to tell of all the daisychains and cowslipballs made by the children under the big elmtree that grew on their mother's lawn; or how they gathered ripe blackberries in autumn; or in the glowing days of summer played about the haycocks, and buried one another in the hay. Their lives were thoughtless and gay, like those of the sparrows in the garden, or the merry little squirrels in the wood.

But a time came at last when these careless days must end. Dame Desley had to take a long journeyshe would be absent for many a monthand on the evening before her departure she called her four children around her.

"My dear children," she said, "I must leave you; I must give you up for a while to the care of another. But I have chosen a guardian for you who is worthy of all your respect. Mr. Learning is coming to see you tomorrow, just an hour before I start; and I hope that he will find you all good and obedient children during my absence. Whatever he may bid you do, do for the love of me, and when you attend to Mr. Learning, think that you are pleasing your mother."

When the four children were alone together, just before going to rest, they began eagerly to talk over what Dame Desley had told them.

"I wonder whether I shall like this Mr. Learning," said Dick, a merry, intelligent boy, with bright eyes that were always twinkling with fun. None of his age could excel him in racing or running; he could climb a tree like a squirrel, and clear a haycock with a bound. He loved the free careless life which he had led in his mother's home, but still he wished for one more full of adventure and excitement.

"I'm quite sure that I shall not like Mr. Learning," cried Matty; "for I have seen him two or three times, and I did not fancy his looks at all. He is as solemn and as grave as an owl; he wears spectacles, and has a very long nose, and his back is as stiff as a poker." Matty was a pretty little girl, with blue eyes, and golden curls hanging down her neck, but she had a conceited air, which spoiled her looks to my mind.

"I wish that we could stay where we are, and go on as we always have done, without being plagued by Mr. Learning at all," cried Lubin, with a weary yawn. Such a fat little fellow as he was, just the shape of a rolypoly pudding, with cheeks as red as the apples that grew on the trees in the orchard.

"But mother spoke kindly of him," said Nelly, a pale lame child who sat in the corner of the room, stringing buttercups and daisies; "if she likes him, should not we try to like him, and not set our hearts against what mother thinks for our good."

"Perhaps Mr. Learning's company may be pleasant for a change!" cried Dick. "I hear that he gives lots of presents to his friends, and makes them both rich and great. It would be a stupid thing, after all, to spend all one's life in gathering wildflowers, or kicking up one's heels in the hay. I mean to be famous one day, and they say there's no way of being so without the help of old Learning. There's Mr. Sharp that lives at the hall; his beautiful house and grounds, his carriages, horses and dogs, all came from Mr. Learning. I've heard of people who, when they were boys, were so poor that they hardly had bread to eat, whom Mr. Learning took under his care, and now they've lots of good things of every sort and kind. Sometimes they're asked to dine with the Lord Mayor of London, where they feast upon turtle and champagne"

Fat little Lubin opened wide both his eyes and mouth on hearing of this.

"And sometimes," continued Dick, "they are actually invited to court, being high in the favour of the Queen."

"I should like to go to court," said Matty, "and wear fine feathers and lace. But I wonder if Mr. Learning will think of doing such grand things for us."

"We will see!" cried the merry Dick; "I'm resolved to get on in the world!" and he turned head over heels at once, as a beginning to his onward progress.

"My children, it is time to go to rest," said the voice of Dame Desley at the door. "Remember to be up in good time in the morning, for my worthy friend Mr. Learning is to breakfast with me tomorrow."

Off went the children to bed. Dick lay awake for some time, thinking over what was before him, and when his merry eyes closed at last in sleep, the subject haunted him still. He dreamed that he was climbing up a little hillock, made of nothing but books of all the colours of the rainbowpurple, and orange, and blueand each book that he looked at had his name as its author in big gilt letters on the back. On the top of the hillock stood Mr. Learning, holding a finelybound volume in one hand, while he held out the other to Dick to help him on in his climbing. Very proud and very joyful was the little boy in his dream as he clambered higher and higher, and thought what a famous figure he was going to make in the world! But what was his delight when Mr. Learning placed the wellbound book in his hand, and on opening it he found that all its leaves were made of fivepound notes!

"Why, I shall be as rich as Crœsus, and as famous as all the seven wise men of Greece put together!" cried Dick, cutting a caper at the top of his hillock in such a transport of joy, that he knocked over the whole pile of books, just as if it had been a house made of cards, and came down flat on his face with such a bang, that it startled him out of his dream.

Back to contents

CHAPTER II.

MR. LEARNING AT BREAKFAST.

LITTLE Nelly, though weak and lame, was the first of the children to come down to the parlour in the morning to help her mother, Dame Desley, to lay the table for breakfast. The child felt a little frightened at the idea of the stranger guest, and doubted whether with all her best efforts she could ever please Mr. Learning.

White were the round breakfast rollsand whiter still the tablecloth on which they were laid; and merrily sang the kettle on the hob, as the white steam rose from its spout.

"Why are there two teapots?" asked Matty, who had just come into the parlour, dressed out in the finest style, as a visitor was expected.

"The larger one is for us, my dear," said her mother, as she went to the cupboard for tea; "and out of the little squareshaped one I shall help my friend Mr. Learning."

Matty was so curious to know why Mr. Learning should have a whole teapot to himself, that she kept hanging about the table, touching the plates, jingling the cups and saucers, and not noticing Dick and Lubin, who had just come into the room.

Dame Desley filled the large teapot, first putting in tea, and afterwards hot water, after the usual fashion; she then went again to the cupboard, and bringing out a dumpy stone bottle, to the amazement of Matty filled the little teapot with ink.

"Now, my dear," she said, turning to Nelly, who stood behind ready to help her, "bring from my desk a quire of foolscap paper, put it on yonder plate, and place a good steel pen beside it. Mr. Learning has a very peculiar taste; instead of tea, toast and butter, he always breakfasts on paper and ink."

"Paper and ink!" echoed all the children; "what a very funny fellow he must be."

"No wonder he's thin!" cried Lubin, opening his round eyes very wide.

"Hush! here he comes," said Dame Desley, going herself to open the door for her honoured guest.

Mr. Learning entered with a solemn air; he was tall, thin, and grave. He had a forehead very broad and very high, and was bald at the top of his head. Thick bushy brows overhung his eyes, which looked calmly through the spectacles which rested on his nose, and a long beard descended from his chin.

The children received their mother's guest each in a different way. Dick, who had made up his mind that Mr. Learning would procure for him fortune and fame, gave him such a long hearty shake that it seemed as if the boy meant to wring off his hand! Lubin, with a pouting air, held out his fat fist when desired by his mother to bid the gentleman "goodmorning." Matty, hanging her head on one side with a very affected air, touched his fingers with the tips of her own. Poor Nelly, who was more shy and timid than the rest, dared not lift up her eyes as she obeyed her mother's command; but she was cheered when the formidable Mr. Learning said in a pleasant voice, "I hope that we shall all be very good friends when we understand each other better."

Then all sat down to breakfast. None of the childrenexcept Lubin, who always thought eating and drinking a very important affaircould attend much to their meal, they watched with such surprise and amusement the movements of Mr. Learning. Helping himself to his inky draught with a pen, which he used instead of a spoon, he then devoured sheet after sheet of foolscap paper with such evident relish, that Dick could hardly help bursting out into a laugh, and Matty was inclined to titter. Mr. Learning used a penwiper instead of a napkin, which saved Dame Desley's linen. He ate his breakfast with a thoughtful air, hardly speaking a single word. When the repast was ended, all arose from the table, and the dame, with a sigh, prepared to bid a long goodbye to her children.

"I leave you under good care, my darlings," said she; "and I expect on my return to find you wiser, happier, and better from the instructions of Mr. Learning, who will show you the little homes provided for you, and teach you how to furnish them. Mind that you do all that he bids you do; work with cheerful goodwill, you will then have reason all your lives to rejoice that you ever knew such a friend. And one more parting word, my children: beware all of the society of Pride; I know that he is lurking about in this neighbourhood, but keep him ever out of your homes."

The children were sorry to part with their mother; lame Nelly was especially sorry. The tears rose into the little girl's eyes, but she hastily wiped them away, and tried to look cheerful and hopeful, that she might not sadden her mother.

Back to contents

CHAPTER III.

THE COTTAGES OF HEAD.

“COME with me, my young friends," said Mr. Learning, as soon as Dame Desley had departed; "I will take you to the four little cottages that have been bought for you by your mother, and which you are, by my help, to furnish with all things needful."

"A cottage all to myselfwhat fun!" exclaimed Dick, cutting a caper on the grass.

Guided by Mr. Learning, the four children went on their way towards the villas of Head, four tiny dwellings that stood close together on the top of a hill, two looking to the east and two to the west. Nice little cottages they were, each with a small garden behind it. The two that fronted the west were thatched with goldencoloured straw, and the glass in the little windows was almost as blue as the sky. The two that looked to the east had darker thatch and brown glass windows. The first were for Matty and Nelly, the others for Lubin and Dick.

"Mine is the prettiest, much the prettiest cottage!" exclaimed Matty, with a smile of delight; "it has the brightest thatch, and the whitest wall, and the most elegant shape besides!"

"Mine is the biggest!" cried Dick with some pride.

Now each of the cottages of Head had two little doors, the funniest that ever were seen; they were just of the form of ears, and Matty's and Nelly's were almost hidden by the golden thatch above them. The children went in and examined the inside of the dwellings one by one. Each had four little roomsparlour, bedroom, kitchen, and spare room. But the walls were quite rough and bare; not a scrap of carpet covered the boards; there were chimneys, it is true, but no grates were to be seen in the empty fireplaces.

"Well," cried Dick, as with his companions he returned to the space between the cottages, in which they had left Mr. Learning standing, "I should be mighty sorry to have to live in such an unfurnished house!"

"If it remain unfurnished it will be your own fault," replied Mr. Learning, as he drew from his pocket four purses, yellow, red, and pink, and blue. "These are the magic purses of Time," he continued, "and most valuable gifts are they; each of you shall possess one. Every morning you will find in them a certain number of pieces of silver and copper money,men name them hours and minutes. A few you will employ in paying for your lodging and food in that large dwelling hard by, called Needful House, in which you may remain for a while until your cottages are fit to be lived in. Some of your hours and minutes you must spend on every weekday in buying furniture for these little Heads in the town of Education."

Dick caught eagerly at the yellow purse, and instantly began to count out the money. Every bright coin had the stamp of a pair of wings on one side, with the motto, "Time flies fast," and on the other side in raised letters the motto, "Use me well."

Lubin and Matty took the red and pink purses with a careless air, as, like too many amongst us, they did not know their value. Lame Nelly very gratefully received the blue purse, with the hours and minutes in it.

"And now," cried Dick, "where is this town of Education, for I'm in a desperate hurry to begin to furnish my Head?"

Mr. Learning moved a few steps to the right, and pointed with his goldheaded cane to a spot where some smoke rising in the valley showed that a large town must be.

"You can see it yonder through the trees," said the sage.

"Oh, dear! it is a good way off!" said Lubin. "I hope that you don't expect us to travel there every day."

"You must not only travel there," replied Mr. Learning, "but you must carry back the things which you purchase, without minding the trouble or fatigue. The way is very straight and direct. You must go down this hill, which is called Puzzle; it is not long, but tolerably steep: you must cross the brook Bother which flows at the bottom, and then the shady lane of Trouble will take you right to the town."

"And what must we do when we get there?" asked Dick.

"Your first care, of course, must be to paper your rooms; each one must do that for himself. The paper you will buy with your money from the decorators, Messrs. Reading and Writing; their house is the first that you will reach when you come to the end of the lane. Then you will doubtless look out for grates, and other needful articles of hardware; they may be had at reasonable prices from Mr. Arithmetic, the ironmonger. Mr. History, the carpetmanufacturer, has a large assortment to show; and General Knowledge, the carpenter, keeps a wonderful variety of beds, tables, and chairs, of every quality and size."

"And our gardens, too, will want looking after," cried Dick.

"Mr. Geography, the nurseryman, will help you to lay them out according to the newest design. You, my young friends," continued Mr. Learning, turning towards the two little girls, "who have garden walls with a western aspect, on which the fruittrees of needlework can grow, must buy plants from Mrs. Sewing, whose white cottage you plainly can see, just at the other side of the brook, near where those weeping willows are dipping their branches in the stream."

"We shall have lots to do with our money," sighed Lubin.

"But quite enough of money for all that you require, if you only do not throw it away, nor let some quickfingered thief like Procrastination steal away your treasure of Time," replied Mr. Learning with a smile. "Think of the pleasure which it will give your mother if she find each of you, on her return six months hence, comfortably settled in a wellfurnished house of your own! If any additional motive for exertion be needed, know that when your mother comes back, I will present a beautiful silver crown of Success to whichever of you four shall have best employed your money in furnishing your garden and house."

"That crown shall be mine!" thought Dick; "I'll win it and wear it too!"

"I shall certainly never get a crown," said Nelly Desley half aloud; "it is quite enough for me if my mother be pleased with my cottage!" A fear was on the little girl's mind that she should manage her shopping very badly, and she hoped that the brook would be shallow, as she could see no bridge across it.

"I shall take my time about this furnishing," said Lubin, as soon as Mr. Learning had taken his departure, promising to return some day to watch the progress of his charges. Lubin, though not lame like Nelly, was heavy and slow in his movements, and often was laughed at by Dick for his great dislike to trouble.

"My cottage looks so pretty outside," said silly little Matty, shaking her fair locks, "that I almost think it would do without any furnishing at all."

Back to contents

CHAPTER IV.

PLAINWORK AND FANCYWORK.

ILL take the measure of my walls at once," cried Dick, "and see what quantity of paper I shall have to buy from Mr. Reading. Shall I look after yours too?" and he turned goodnaturedly to his sisters.

"Please do, dear Dick," replied Nelly.

"I shall leave Master Lubin to measure his own; a lazy young urchin like him would not move a finger if he could help it; I would not give one of my minutes for his chance of winning the crown of Success!"

"I shall do very well," grumbled Lubin, not much pleased at the cutting remark.

"Matty, dear," said Nelly to her sister, "as we have something to buy that our brothers have notand plants of needlework, mother says, are best when put in at the beginning of springhad we not better set off at once and buy what Mr. Learning recommended? Mrs. Sewing does not live far off; we might carry up our needlework plants before our brothers are ready to start with us for the town of Education."

"You are always in a hurry!" cried Matty.

"It is because I am lame," replied Nelly meekly; "as I can never go fast, I am obliged to make up for my slowness by starting early."

"Well, it's a fine bright morning, and it's rare fun to have a run down hill!" cried Matty, "so I am quite willing to go."

Off she flew like a bird, her long ringlets streaming behind her, and her merry laugh was borne back by the wind to Nelly, who, at a much slower pace, walked carefully down the hill. As Matty, however, took to chasing a bright butterfly, which led her quite out of her way, Nelly was the first to reach the brook which flowed at the bottom of the hill. To her great comfort she found that there were steppingstones across it, so that there was no need that she should wet her feet with the waters of Bother. Mrs. Sewing's house was also quite near, so that there was little trouble in reaching it.

The good woman herself was outside her door, occupied in training a large plant of needlework over her porch.

"Goodmorning," said Nelly, who had slowly picked her way over the steppingstones of the brook.

"Goodmorning," repeated Matty, who had rushed on, out of breath with her haste, that she might not be behind her sister.

Mrs. Sewing was a prim little dame, dressed in a curious garment of patchwork, with a necklace of small round pincushions hanging almost as low as her waist. Instead of her own hair she wore a most singular wig, made entirely of skeins of cotton and wool, which hung a long way down her back.

She received her young customers with a low formal courtesy, and said with a smile as she turned from the one to the other,

"That girl is wise, and worth the knowing,
Who in life's springtime comes to sewing."
"Mrs. Sewing," said Matty, who could hardly refrain from laughing at the funny appearance of the prim old lady, "we've come to buy plants of needlework from you to train up our garden walls. We've plenty of money to buy them with,"here she jingled her hours and minutes,"so pray show us your stock directly, for we're in haste to begin our planting."

With another courtesy Mrs. Sewing made reply,

"I've Runningup and Fellingdown,
And Hemming for a lady's gown;
I've Buttonhole, and Herringbone,
And Stitching, finest ever known;
I've Whipping that will cause no crying,
And Basting, never source of sighing;
For good Plainwork, there's no denying,
Is always worth a woman's trying."
"I don't much admire these Plainwork plants," said Matty, with rather a discontented air; "their blossoms are so miserably small, the leaves are so big, and the stems are all set with thorns, just as sharp as needles. You have something yonder a thousand times prettier, with flowers of every hue, and in such lovely little pots!" and Matty pointed as she spoke to a row of plants of Fancywork, that were at no great distance.

Again Mrs. Sewing courtesied and replied,

"I've Knitting, Netting, Crochet, Tatting,

I've Beadwork, Germanwork, and Plaiting,
I've Tentstitch, Crossstitch, Stitches various
To show off patterns multifarious;
Round Fancywork each lady lingers,
So please your taste and ply your fingers."
"There now!" exclaimed Matty, who, followed by Nelly, had eagerly run to the Fancywork row; "was ever anything so pretty as this! Every blossom like bunches of beads that glitter so brightly in the sun! This, this is the plant for my money; and then it is so easy to be carried!"

Nelly also looked with great admiration on the beautiful flower, and felt greatly inclined to choose one like it. She knew that she had not hours enough to purchase all that she might like, and it was quite natural in a little girl to wish for what was pretty and pleasant. But a thought crossed the lame child's mind, and laying her hand on Matty's arm, she whispered in her sister's ear: "Don't you remember, dear, how fond mother is of the fruits of Plainwork; we've heard her say many a time that no Fancywork in the world is half so much to her liking. Now mother will come back to us again when the fruit will have had time to ripen; pretty blossoms are nice to look at; but the great thing, after all, is the fruit."

"I'm not going to plague myself with that stupid Plainwork," cried Matty, shrugging her shoulders; "but it may do for you!" She said this in so scornful a tone that it brought the colour to Nelly's pale cheek.

"Why should I mind?" thought the lame little girl; "I know that mother likes Plainwork best; she values things that are useful rather than those that are pretty; and oh, I'm so glad that she does so, or what would become of me!"

So Matty purchased the pretty ornamented creeper, with its clusters of brightcoloured beads, and Nelly took a fine thriving plant of Plainwork, to train up her garden wall.

Then both took leave of Mrs. Sewing, who, smiling and courtesying to the girls, bade them farewell in these words,

"Pleasure and profit both attend ye,
Sewing ever shall befriend ye!"
Matty's plant was in a small light pot, and she easily carried it across the brook; then turning, she looked back at her sister, who could hardly see the steppingstones through the thick leaves of the plant which she bore. Nelly's pot was also very heavy, and before she could reach the shore, her lame foot slipped on a stone, and she fell splash into the waters of Bother.

The stream was very shallow, so there was no danger of her being drowned, but the shock, the tumble, and the wetting were anything but agreeable. It was very unkind in Matty to stand, as she did, laughing at her poor lame sister, as she floundered in the brook of Bother, still grasping her pot of Plainwork.

"Oh, dear, dear! how the thornneedles are pricking my fingers!" gasped Nelly.

"Then let gothrow the stupid Plainwork away," cried Matty.

But Nelly had too brave a spirit for that. She knew that what was worth acquiring was worth bearing, and she would not be discouraged by a trifle. I wish that some of my little readers who sit pouting and fretting over a seam, crying over a broken needle, or a prick on a tiny finger, could have seen Nelly when, with repeated efforts, she scrambled out of the brook, with Plainwork safe in her grasp.

The two girls now made their way up the hill of Puzzle, on their return to the cottages of Head. Matty, eager to plant her pretty creeper, greatly outstripped her sister, as she had done when they at first had set out. But with patient, uncomplaining labour, Nelly Desley plodded on her course, and before long both Plainwork and Fancywork were safely transplanted into the ground by the wall at the back of the gardens.

Nelly could hardly see the steppingstones through the thick leaves of the plant which she bore.
Page .

CHAPTER V.

MR. ALPHABET.

NOW we're all ready to set off to Messrs. Reading and Writing," cried Dick, as the four children stood together on the slope of the hill; "I vote we have a raceone, two, three, off and away!" and dashing forward like a young stag, he rushed down the hill, distancing even Matty, and with the force of his own rapid descent cleared brook Bother at a bound.

Nelly could not help clapping her hands.

"I should have thought," observed fat Lubin, who had kept at her side, "that you, of all people in the world, would have hated this silly racing, and disliked to see any one go at so desperate a pace."

"Why should I dislike it?" asked the lame child; "I would go at a great pace too, if I only were able."

"But when you are lame, does it not vex you to be so distanced by others?"

Nelly hesitated a little before she replied, "Sometimes, I own, it does vex me a little; but then I am comforted when I think that as long as I do my best I should be only glad that others can do better."

Lubin and Nelly came up with their brother and sister at the cottage of Mrs. Sewing; for Dick, who was in a merry mood, had stopped there to help the old dame to transplant a fine slip of Fancywork, and Matty was standing laughing beside him.

"See how well he does it!" she cried.

"I wonder that he is not ashamed to use his fingers like a girl!" exclaimed Lubin, who was himself remarkably clumsy.

Mrs. Sewing turned round with a smile and a courtesy.

"Better the fingers thus employing
Than in fighting, fidgeting, or destroying,"
observed she.

Dick looked up and laughed. "I'll soon prove to you, my lad," he cried, "that hands that can ground a pretty slip of German work, are ready and fit for something harder," and he squared up towards Lubin with clenched fists, and such a merry look of defiance, that his brother was more than convinced by the sight, and trotted off along the lane of Trouble, at a much brisker pace than usual.

"We'll go after the plump one," cried Dick, "or he'll arrive at Mr. Reading's before us."

Along the lane they all went. The weather had been dry of late, and the road was not so muddy as usual. Indeed the walk was so agreeable that Dick remarked that "trouble is a pleasure." It was not long before the four young householders found themselves at the door of Messrs. Reading and Writing.

Their shop was a very large and handsome one; indeed a finer and better was not to be seen in the whole town of Education, on the outskirts of which it stood. It was separated into two divisions, over the first and principal of which Mr. Reading himself presided. A great variety of papers for walls were displayed in the large glass windows, and when the children peeped in they saw a vast number more in the shop.

"Well, here's a fine choice!" exclaimed Matty, in pleased surprise; "I think that one might spend half one's life in the shop of Mr. Reading, and always find out something pretty and new."

"But where is Mr. Reading himself?" cried Lubin; "and how are we to get through this iron grating which shuts us out from the shop?"

His last question was answered by the funniest little dwarf that ever was seen, who popped out from behind the counter, and with a large iron key in his hand came toddling up to the grating. He was just twentysix inches high, and had a head almost as big as the rest of his body.

"I say, little chap, will you let us in?" said Dick, rapping on the iron bars.

"I'm not accustomed to be spoken to after that fashion," cried the dwarf angrily; "my name is not 'little chap,' but 'Mr. Alphabet,' though some dare to call me A B C. I ought to be treated with respect, for I am several thousand years old."

"You've been wondrously slow then in your growth," laughed Lubin; "I think I could jump over your head."

"It's easier said than done," grumbled Alphabet, casting up a glance of scorn at the boy, whose fat figure was not formed for jumping; "and I should advise you to have a care how you provoke me by any boasting or insolent language. I am both strong and bold, and I come of an ancient race. My father was an Egyptian, or a Phœnician, or"

"Never mind your father just now, my good fellow," cried Dick; "just turn your key in the lock, and let us into the shop of Mr. Reading."

"You don't suppose that I'm going to let you pass without paying toll," growled Alphabet; "I always expect a fee of some of the money of Time."

"Let us in," cried Lubin, kicking the grating.

"You may kick till you're tired," said the gruffy little dwarf; "no one gets to Mr. Reading without paying toll to Mr. Alphabet, his highly respectable porter."

"Let's give him his fee and be done with it," cried Matty, hastily pulling out her purse.

Seeing that there was no use in refusing, as Alphabet had the key of the gate, each of the children now produced some money, Dick giving less than the others. Alphabet took the bright hours with a merry grin, as he swung back the iron grating; but when Lubin was about to pass in, the dwarf planted himself in the way.

"You said that you could jump over my head; just try."

"I don't just think that I could," said Lubin, who was daunted by the manner of the dwarf.

"Now, for your stupid boast," growled Alphabet, "I will not allow you to pass till you've paid twice as much as the others have done;" and as he spoke he half closed the grating in Lubin's face.

"You can't keep me out now you've unlocked it," cried Lubin (who was, however, still on the outside, having been as usual behindhand), and he tried to push the gate open.

"Push away," said the dwarf with a grin.

But poor Lubin soon found to his cost that Alphabet was strong as well as little, and quite able to hold his own against any amount of pushing.

"Won't you help me?" cried Lubin to Dick; the fat boy was getting quite red with his efforts.

"Oh, nonsense; fair play is a jewel!" exclaimed Dick; "you must fight it out for yourself. If you can't master little A B C, a precious poor creature you must be."

"Pay double toll, or I'll never let you in!" shouted the passionate dwarf.

There was no help for it; poor Lubin was obliged to pull out his money; and Alphabet, with a grin of triumph, at last allowed him to enter.

"Is Mr. Reading at home?" asked Dick.

"He is just within," said the dwarf; "if you'll look over the papers for a minute, I'll go and tell him that you are waiting."

Back to contents

CHAPTER VI.

MR. READING'S FINE SHOP.

WELL, Mr. Reading keeps a splendid assortment indeed!" exclaimed Dick, looking round the immense shop with delight. "There are such lots of fine papers here that the only difficulty will be which to choose!"

"I know what I will choose!" cried Matty; "that paper all covered with pretty little fairies!"

"It is but a poor paper; I cannot in conscience recommend it for wear," said Mr. Reading, who at that instant made his appearance from an inner part of the shop.

"Oh, but it is charming!" cried Matty; "I should care for no paper like that."

"And I see what I like best!" exclaimed Dick; "there's the jolliest paper that ever was made; don't you see it, up in that corner?sets of cannibals dancing round a fire!"

"That's the Robinson Crusoe pattern," observed Mr. Reading, "a great favourite with young customers of mine."

"That's the paper for my money!" cried Dick; "I never saw anything more to my mind!"

Nelly and Lubin then chose their patterns, the former thinking what would please the taste of her mother, the latter what would cost least of his Time money; for the lazy rogue grudged every hour that he gave to reading.

A difficulty came into Nelly's mind. "We are to paper our rooms ourselves," said she; "how can we do so, having nothing with which we can fasten the paper on firmly?"

"I've the paste of Attention at your service," said Reading; "you will find nothing more certain to stick on a paper than that. You shall carry home a can of it today."

"And there is another thing which we must remember," observed Lubin, who had a sensible and reflecting mind, though too lazy to make much use of it; "as our walls are higher of course than ourselves, we must have a ladder to lift us to the higher parts of them."

"I can supply that want also," cried the ready Mr. Reading, who seemed to take pleasure in serving his young guests; "I've the magic ladder of Spelling, and I am willing to let it on hire."

"Let's see this ladder," said Dick.

At a word from his master, Alphabet, the stout little dwarf, withdrew into an inner part of the dwelling, and soon reappeared, lugging with him a ladder which was three times as long as himself.

"This is a very curious and ingenious ladder," remarked Mr. Reading, "and quite worthy of your closest observation. You see that on the under part of each step is a sentence quite perfectly spelt; but this, of course, cannot be seen when the ladder is placed by a wall. On the upper part appears the same sentence, but with many a blunder in it to try your powers of recollection. You must study the ladder well before you attempt to mount it, and get the right spelling fixed in your mind, so as to make no mistakes. Then, before putting your foot upon any step, you must spell the sentence upon it; if you correct every blunder, the wood will be firm as a rock; but if you leave a single fault unnoticed, one little letter misplaced, the step will give way under your weight, and land you flat on the floor."

"What a horrible ladder!" exclaimed Lubin; "it seems to have been expressly contrived to break the neck of every one who is so silly as to mount it."

"It only needs care in the using," replied polite Mr. Reading, unable to suppress a quiet smile; while Alphabet, who thought it a capital joke, burst into a loud laugh. "I confess that the ladder of Spelling has been the cause of many a tumble; but still it is an excellent ladder,the trees of which it was made grew beside our own stream of Bother."

"Any one might have guessed that!" muttered Lubin, rubbing his head with a disconsolate air, as if he already felt the bumps produced by the ladder of Spelling.

"Let's see these funny sentences on the steps," said Dick, "that we are forced to spell so finely. Such a comical ladder as this will make the papering of our walls a very slow affair."

As my readers may be curious to know whether they could have mounted the ladder without any step breaking beneath them, I will give them a few of the sentences to correct at their leisure. I write the faulty words in italics, though I hope that it is not needful to do so.

I hav to ants, too unkels to,
The kindest wons I ever new.
Except this presint, nevew deer,
I am sow glad to here your hear.
Gals sow shurts, and boys sew beens,
Labour is scene in various seens.
I eat ate appels at a fate,
Then took my leve and warked home strait.
The winds they blue; the sky was blew;
Tom, as they dashed the oshon threw,
Write overbored a poney through.
Our sovrin rains in joy and piece;
The summer reigns our crops increese;
The weery horse from rain release.
"I tell you what I'll do," said Lubin, after thoughtfully surveying the ladder from the top to the bottom: "I'll get goodnatured little Nelly to stand below while I'm climbing the steps, and she shall call out to me the right spelling, so that I shall be certain to make no blunder."

Polite Mr. Reading shook his head. "Each must master the difficulty for himself," he replied; "not a single step would keep firm were there any attempt at such prompting."

Poor Lubin heaved a sigh like a groan.

"Who's afraid!" exclaimed Dick; "the greater the difficulty the greater the glory of mounting to the top of the ladder! Just roll up our papers, Mr. Reading, we'll carry them under our arms. The girls will take charge of the can of paste, and as for this remarkable ladder, Lubin and I will contrive to bear it between us."

Thus loaded, the little party passed again through the iron grating. Dick walked first, with a confident air, holding one end of the ladder of Spelling, while Lubin, grumbling and sighing, supported the other end. Nelly followed with the can of Attention, for Matty was too much engaged in looking at and admiring her pretty fairy paper to think of her lame little sister. Mr. Reading, the most polite and agreeable of shopkeepers, bade them farewell with a bow; and little Alphabet shouted after Lubin, "When you can manage to get to the top of the ladder of Spelling without tumbling down on your nose, I'll give you free leave to come back and jump over my head if you like it!"

Back to contents

CHAPTER VII.

THE LADDER OF SPELLING.

WHAT a jolly pleasant fellow old Reading is!" cried Dick, as they jogged along.

"Well enough," replied Lubin, jerking his shoulder, "if he had not plagued us with this hateful ladder, and did not keep such a covetous, impudent little porter as that ugly old dwarf A B C."

"I did not see much harm in the dwarf," laughed Dick; "the best fun I ever had in my life was seeing you pushing on one side of the gate, and the little chap pushing on the other. Alphabet was too hard for you, Lubin, my boy, though he is such a mite of a man."

The observation made Lubin rather sulky, and he said nothing till, having passed through the lane of Trouble, the party stopped by the brook of Bother.

"I'm afraid, Lubin," observed Dick, "that an awkward fellow like you may miss your footing if attempting to cross while carrying a weight on your shoulder. You go first, unburdened, and then I'll easily stretch out the end of the ladder for you to catch hold of."

Lubin did not wait to be twice invited to put down his tiresome burden. He flung down his end of the ladder, went across the steppingstones at once, and then, without so much as turning to look at his companion, began to walk fast up the hill.

"Holloa! stop! where are you going?" shouted Dick.

Lubin only quickened his pace.

"The lazy rogue means to leave me to carry this ladder all by myself!" exclaimed Dick, in high indignation.

"I wish that I could help you, dear Dick," said Nelly; "but I'm lame, and"

"And you've been carrying the can all the way, till your face is quite pale with fatigue. I wonder that that saucy puss Matty is not ashamed of treating you so."

"I was so busy with my fairies that I forgot," began Matty.

"Ah, well; take the can now and remember. And as for the ladder" Without finishing his sentence, to the surprise of the girls, Dick suddenly turned round, and walked back several paces. His object soon became plain; he was giving himself room for a run. Once more he rushed forward with a bound, and, laden as he was with ladder and with paper, was over the brook in a moment.

"There's a jump!" he exclaimed, his face flushed less with the effect, than with the pride which he felt in having accomplished such a feat; "depend on't, a boy who can leap like that won't soon be turned back in life's long race by any difficulty or trial. I only wish that Mr. Learning could have seen me take that jump."

Nelly's admiration of her brother's remarkable powers was a little damped by a fear that arose in her mind when she saw how he gloried in them. Nelly was very fond of Dick, but she could not help thinking that she would rather have seen him conquer his pride than jump over halfadozen Bothers. Slowly and thoughtfully the little girl passed over the brook, and Matty, who was now carrying the can, brought up the rear of the party.

"Dick," said Matty, when she had joined her brother, "I wonder that you did not lay the ladder of Spelling across the stream, and make a bridge of it at once."

"I was too wary a bird for that," laughed Dick. "You know I've not yet mastered that awkward spelling, and if I'd put my foot upon a step, I should just have gone souse into Bother."

"Oh, I quite forgot!" exclaimed Matty.

"You seem to have a trick of forgetting," said her brother; "you forget that your can of Attention is full, and you swing it to and fro as you walk, so that you spill it at every step. You had better give it up again to Nelly."

"How Lubin trots up the hill!" cried Matty. "I never thought that he could get on so fast."

"He knows pretty well what he has to expect when I get up with him!" cried Dick, who was indignant at his brother's desertion; "I mean to give the fat rogue such a thrashing as he never had before in his life!"

"Oh no, dear Dick!" exclaimed Nelly. "I am sure that you had better forgive and forget."

"I don't see why I should," rejoined Dick.

"There are a great many reasons," said Nelly, who never suffered an angry or revengeful feeling to rest in her heart; "we know that it is noble and right to forgive, and to do as we would be done by; and has not dear mother a thousand times told us to live in love and kindness together?"

"But he played me such a shabby trick!" exclaimed Dick.

"You must remember, dear brother, that Lubin is not so strong as you are, and cannot bear a weight with such ease."

"No; you're right there!" cried Dick proudly, raising the ladder of Spelling with one hand above his head, to show the might of his arm.

Nelly saw that her brother was getting into better humour, and ventured to say something more. "There is another reason why you should forgive Lubin. Poor Lubin has also, perhaps, something to forgive and forget."

"I never ran off and left him in the lurch."

"No," replied Nelly, in a very gentle tone; "but when he was in trouble with Alphabet, you burst out laughing instead of helping him. I don't think, dear Dick, that you know what pain you give by your way of joking and mocking at others who can't do as much as yourself."

"Have I ever pained you, Nelly?"

"Sometimes," replied the child.

Dick was silent for a few minutes. He was recalling to mind times when he had ridiculed his gentle little sister for her lamenessthe slow pace which she could not avoid. He felt ashamed of his ungenerous conduct, and willing to make some amends.

"It was too bad in me to hurt you, Nelly, who never gave pain to any one; so, for your sake, this time I'll consent to forgive and forget."

While this conversation went on, the brother and sisters had walked halfway up the hill, and, before many minutes had passed, they had all arrived at their group of cottages. Dick kept his word to Nelly, and took no further notice of the desertion of Lubin, than by saying, with a laugh, when first they met, "You went up the hill at such a pace, my fine fellow, that one might have thought that you fancied the terrible Alphabet following close at your heels."

Lubin looked rather sulky, but was glad to be so easily let off; he was not aware that he owed Dick's forbearance to the kindly offices of peacemaker Nelly.

As the day was now far advanced, the children resolved not to begin their papering work till the morrow. They went to the house Needful, where they were to have their board and lodging for a short time, till their cottages should be a little furnished. They were all rather tired with their day's exertions, and none but Dick felt disposed to take a stroll in the evening.

Back to contents

CHAPTER VIII.

BREAKING DOWN.

THE first care of Matty and Nelly in the morning, after they had taken their breakfast, was to water their needlework plants.

"I can't think," said Matty to her sister, "how you could be so silly as to choose that ugly Plainwork,I'm sure there's not a bit of beauty in it."

"I wait for the fruit," said Nelly meekly.

"It does not climb high like mine, to adorn the walls; it creeps heavily along the ground. It is such a meanlooking plant."

"We shall not think it mean in the season of ripening," observed Nelly.

"Ah, here comes Lubin!" cried Matty; "he was late for breakfast, as usual. Goodmorning, my lazy brother. Do you know what has become of Dick?"

"Not I," answered Lubin, with a yawn.

"Perhaps he has been working at his cottage already," said Nelly, "and has been studying the ladder of Spelling. Just wait till I fetch the can of pastewe'll put Attention into several little pots, and all begin papering our walls together."

Nelly soon brought the paste, which she had kept during the night at house Needful. As Lubin and his sisters went towards the group of cottages, they heard the cheerful voice of Dick calling to them from the inside of his own.

"Come in here with you, and I'll show you something worth the seeing."

"Why, Dick," exclaimed Matty, who was the first to enter, "you don't mean to say that you have papered half your parlour already!"

"I don't say it, but you may see it," said Dick.

"What wonderful progress you have made!"

"I should say that I have," returned Dick, with a mighty selfsatisfied air, as he looked around his parlour, already quite gay with the Robinson Crusoe pattern. "I've done more, too, than you can see," he added, striking his hand on the ladder of Spelling, which he had placed by the wall; "I've learned every sentence in this ladder as perfectly as any man can learn them, and can now climb to the very top with the greatest safety and ease."

Matty and Lubin looked on their clever brother with eyes in which admiration seemed mixed with a little envy.

"But how could you paper the room without paste?" exclaimed Nelly; "I had charge of the whole supply."

"My dear simple sister," replied Dick, "you don't suppose that all the paste in the world is held in your can, or that no other kind is to be had. I took a stroll yesterday evening with my acquaintance, young Pride, and he told me of a firstrate paste called Emulation, showed me where to get it, and helped me to lay in a capital store. You've no notion how pleasantly it made me get on with my work. I believe I shall paper all my four rooms before you have finished a single one of yours."

"Oh, let me have some of your paste!" cried Matty.

"Have it and welcome," said Dick; "it's cheap, and there's plenty for all. I don't know what is making our little Nelly look so serious and grave."

"Oh, Dick," said the child, in a hesitating tone, "did not dear mother warn us to have nothing to do with Pride?"

"He's a jolly good fellow!" cried Dick.

"But mother forbade us to keep company with him."

"Really, Nelly," said Dick, rather sharply, "I'm old enough to choose my own friends."

"But if Pride should prove to be not a friend but an enemy? Oh, dear brother, I should be afraid to use anything that Pride recommends."

Dick burst into a laugh. "Use what you like, poor, patient, plodding little pussy; leave me to follow my own ways. You've not resolved, as I have, to win the crown of Success. You were never made to shine, unless it be like some little taper, giving its quiet light in a cottage; while I mean to dazzle the world some day, like the eruption of a splendid volcano."

"A precious lot of mischief you may do," observed Lubin; "better be a sober taper in a cottage, that cheers and gives light to some one, than a blazing volcano, that makes a grand show indeed, but leaves ruins and ashes behind it."

"Every one to his liking!" cried Dick, nimbly mounting the ladder, and spelling over the sentences so fast that his hearers could hardly follow him. Doubtless he meant to show off his talent, but, in his eagerness to be admired, he forgotwho can wonder that he did so?the right spelling of one little word. Down he fell crack on the floor, the moment that he put his foot on the poney!

Up jumped Dick in a second, not hurt indeed, but a good deal mortified, especially as Lubin laughed, and Matty began to titter.

"Here we go up, up, up,
Here we go down, down, down, oh!
That is clever Dick's way
Of winning the silver crown, oh!"
cried Lubin, his fat sides shaking with mirth.

"I would not stand that from him!" exclaimed a voice from without, and the shadow of Pride, a beetlebrowed, blackhaired, illfavoured lad, now darkened the doorway of Dick.

"I'll stand no impudence!" cried Dick in a passion, and, dashing with clenched fist up to Lubin, he knocked him down with a blow.

"Give it him well!" shouted Pride.

But Nelly rushed forward in haste, and threw herself between her two brothers. "Oh, don't, don't!" she cried in distress; "remember our mother, remember the love which we all should bear to one another! It was wrong in Lubin to laughbut oh, pleaseplease don't beat him any more."

"I'll beat him in another way!" exclaimed Dick, who was, perhaps, a little ashamed of having struck his younger brother; "I'll beat him at climbing this ladder,one fall shall never daunt me!" and once more he ascended the steps, spelling without a single blunder, till, on the very topmost round, he waved his hand in triumph.

"I hope you're not hurt?" whispered Nelly to Lubin, who was slowly rising from the ground.

The boy turned gloomily away.

"You don't want her, do you, to cuddle and pet you as if you were a great big baby?" said Pride. "I wonder you don't go to your own cottage, and shut yourself up quietly there."

"I'll go and have nothing more to do with any of them," muttered Lubin, pushing Nelly aside, and leaving the cottage of Dick in a mood by no means amiable.

Nelly sighed; and as it appeared that she could at present be of no more use to her brothers, she quietly took her portion of Attention, and went to paper her own little room.

I shall not tell of all her difficulties and troubles, nor how, when using the ladder of Spelling, she found it several times give way, and drop her down on the floor. The process of learning is a slow one, as every one is likely to know who has done enough of the papering work to be able to read this book;and as for that troublesome ladder, A. L. O. E. will not venture to say that she has never had a tumble from it herself. I need only mention, as regards lame Nelly, that in the end, after days and weeks of patient labour, her house was very neatly papered indeed.

Matty had far less trouble. The ladder of Spelling seemed made on purpose to suit her convenience; she mounted the steps with greater ease than even the active Dick could do. Her walls were soon covered with fairies; but, as Lubin observed, no one could think the cottage of Head well furnished with a paper so poor and thin,you could almost see the bricks through it. Matty was, however, well pleased; and even, in the blindness of selflove, had some hopes of the silver crown. Pride flattered her skill and her quickness, and was always a welcome guest at her cottage as well as in Dick's. Neither the brother nor the sister yet knew the evils that might arise from their using the paste of Emulation.

And how fared poor Lubin meantime? He worked slowly, by fits and starts, whenever the humour was on him, but it seemed to his brother and sisters as if his walls would never be papered. Nelly, after her own day's work, would carry the ladder to Lubin, but he constantly refused to use it.

"What nonsense it is," he would angrily say, "to have words sounded in one way, and spelt in another. I wish that the fellow who made that ladder had been well ducked in the brook of Bother."

"But as it has been made, and we've no other," observed Nelly, "would it not be wise to make the best of it?"

By her gentle persuasion Lubin more than once attempted to mount the first step, but it always gave way beneath him; he never could remember of the to, too, and two, which was the right one to use.

At last, catching up the ladder in despair, Lubin flung it out of his door.

"Let it goI should like to break it to bits and make a bonfire of it!" he cried; "I can paper my rooms without it."

"Oh, no; not the upper parts," suggested Nelly.

"I don't care for the upper parts, I'll leave them as they are," answered Lubin. "If the bricks and mortar are ugly, no one need look at them, say I."

"But, Lubin," exclaimed Matty, who had just come in, "you will be quite ashamed of your house if it be furnished worse than a ploughboy's."

"It will do very well," replied Lubin. "I hate this papering nonsense, and I wish that Mr. Learning had been far enough away, rather than come to plague us poor children with his tiresome Reading and Spelling!"

Back to contents

CHAPTER IX.

MR. LEARNING'S VISIT.

IT must not be supposed that during the time which it took to paper the cottages, other things were neglected; that Plainwork and Fancywork were not watered, or that frequent shopping expeditions were not made to the town of Education. My history is by no means a journal of each day's proceedings, but only an account of some incidents that seem most worthy of note.

I wish that I could tell my young readers that Dick frankly owned himself sorry for having knocked down poor Lubin. Perhaps he would have done so, for he had a kind and generous disposition, but for the evil influence of Pride. This dark companion was almost always now at the elbow of Dick, filling him with notions of his own importance, making him look down upon every one who was not so sharp as himself. From cottage to cottage Pride moved, now putting in Lubin's mind gloomy, angry feelings towards his brother; now flattering the vanity of Matty, till she thought herself a perfect model of beauty and almost too good to keep company with her lame little sister Nelly. Pride did not fail also to try to put evil into Nelly's heart, but she never would let him converse with her; she remembered the words of her mother, and shunned the dark tempter who leads so many astray.

"I wonder," said Pride one day to Matty as she was watering her Fancywork plant,"I wonder why a lovely young creature like you should not spend more of Time's money upon dress."

Matty giggled and blushed, and said that she feared that there was not such a person as a good milliner to be found in all the town of Education.

"Well," said Pride, "I think that I can help you to find one whom no one has ever excelled in this important line of business. There is a distant relation of my own, Miss Folly, who is wonderfully quick with her fingers, and makes all sorts of elegant things. Lady Fashion has her so often with her at her fine townhouse, that it is clear that she regards Miss Folly almost in the light of a friend, and would not know how to get on without her. Folly is particularly anxious to employ her art in hiding any changes made by age. I have known an old lady dressed up by her with wig, rouge, and a low muslin dress, fastened up with bunches of roses, whom you really would have taken, at least at a distance, for some lovely young creature of twenty!"

"Oh, could you not introduce me to Miss Folly!" exclaimed Matty; "if she could so beautify an ugly old lady, what would she do for a young girl like me!"

"I will bring her here with the greatest pleasure," replied Pride; and glancing at Matty's dress, he added, "From the elegant style of your attire, I should have really imagined that you had long ago known Miss Folly."

When Dick had almost finished his papering, and Matty was far advanced with hers, the children received one day a visit from Mr. Learning, who came to observe their progress. Nelly was so hard at work in her spare room, that she did not hear his step, and was a little startled when she felt a heavy hand laid on her shoulder.

"Don't be afraid," said Mr. Learning kindly, "go quietly on with your work. 'Slow and sure' is your motto, I see; what you do is done neatly and nicely."

Nelly looked up with a pleased smile. She had never expected to receive a word of praise from the tall stately gentleman in black, who lived upon paper and ink.

Mr. Learning then proceeded to Matty's cottage. Matty, who happened to be twining flowers in her beautiful hair, started up, and, in a little confusion, greeted her guardian with a courtesy.

He glanced round the cottage for awhile in silence. Matty thought that he must be admiring the quickness with which she had papered her walls; his first words disappointed her not a little.

"You have made a great mistake in not choosing a better and stronger paper; labour is thrown away upon this. However quickly you may get over your work, no one will ever think a dwelling wellfurnished whose walls are covered with nothing but fairies."

"Stupid, solemn, crossgrained old critic as he is!" thought Matty; "I knew that he and I would never agree together. I paper my walls to please my own taste, and snap my fingers at Learning!"

The grave guardian then stalked slowly across the little plot of ground which divided the boys' cottages from those of the girls. Though Dick's was just opposite to Matty's, Mr. Learning chose to cross over first to Lubin's.

The boy, buried in a deep slumber, lay snoring upon the floor, quite unconscious that any one had entered. With great disgust Mr. Learning looked around on one of the most untidy rooms that his eyes had ever beheld. It was only papered to such a height as the arm of the fat boy could reach, and even the little that had been done had been finished in the very worst way. So small a quantity of the paste of Attention had been used, that the paper was already falling off; odd pieces were lying here and there, and the most careless observer must have seen that he was in the dwelling of a sluggard.

Mr. Learning said nothing at all; he did not even waken the sleeping boy, though he felt a little inclined to give him a poke with his boot. The stately guardian took out from his pocket a piece of chalk, and wrote on the rough bricks above the paper, in letters half a foot high, the single word dunce, then turning round on his heel, he quitted the cottage of Lubin.

It was perhaps intentionally that the sage had arranged to make his visit to Dick the last. Here there was much to satisfy and please his philosophic eye, and Mr. Learning's grave face relaxed into a smile as pleasant as if a whole dozen of copybooks had been spread out for dinner before him.

"You're a clever fellow," said he; and Dick made a very low bow, pleased but not at all surprised by the compliment.

"I should not wonder if, some day," pursued Mr. Learning, "I should be able to introduce you to my friends the Ologies."

"Pray, who may they be?" asked Dick; "I never heard of them before."

"They are of a remarkably superior family, that has been settled for a length of years in the higher part of the town of Education. There are a number of brothers, and they are all remarkable men. There's

"The Ology, who keeps a religious library;

"Myth Ology, who deals in books describing the superstitions of heathen nations;

"Ge Ology, whose collection of marbles, stones, various earths, and old fossils makes him famous;

"Phren Ology, who professes to tell the characters of people by feeling the bumps on their heads;

"Chron Ology, who manufactures nails that are known by the name of dates;

"Conch Ology, who keeps a museum with a vast variety of shells;

"Entom Ology, who has another filled with butterflies and other insects;

"Ichthy Ology, whose taste leads him to make a collection of fish;

"Zo Ology, who has a large garden with all kinds of creatures in it."

"What a very large family it is!" exclaimed Dick, who had begun to think that these Ologies would never come to an end.

"I have not mentioned all," replied Learning. "But all are intimate friends of mine, and I invite them all every year to a feast in my house in London."

"I wonder what you give them to eat!" thought Dick, "and whether these Ologies have all your own taste for paper and ink!" He had a little awe for Mr. Learning, so did not utter the reflection aloud.

"You shall know them all some day," continued the guardian; "they will help you to fortune and to fame!"

"Why not know them at once?" cried Dick.

Mr. Learning smiled again; but this time his smile was not so pleasant. "You are by far too young," he replied, "and have something else to think of at present. Your cottage is nearly papered, I see, but you have as yet not a single grate within it."

"I'm going to the ironmonger's this very day," cried Dick; "there's no use in waiting for my brother and sisters, they are so slow at their work. I shall be hand and glove with all the Ologies before Lubin has covered his ugly bricks!"

What was Mr. Learning looking at so attentively through his spectacles, as Dick uttered this sounding boast? He had caught a glimpse of Pride, who, upon his entrance, had hidden himself behind the open door, and who was there listening to the conversation between Dick and his guardian.

"Let me give you one word of advice, my boy," said Mr. Learning, in a serious tone; "go to the town of Education as often as you will, and buy what you may, but never let Pride go with you. He is a safe companion for no one; and the better that you are acquainted with me, the less cause you will find to cherish him!" and with this quiet warning, Mr. Learning quitted the cottage.

"Ah, Pride!" cried Dick, as the dark one sneaked out of his hidingplace behind the door; "you find that the saying is true, 'Listeners never hear good of themselves.'"

Pride looked offended and annoyed.

"Never mind, old friend," continued Dick; "I won't attend to a word that he said, for I find you as pleasant a companion as any that ever I knew. I'm just going off to the town to buy grates from Arithmetic the Ironmonger, and if you like to come with me, I can but say that you'll be heartily welcome."

Pride needed no second invitation, and the two soon started together.

Back to contents

CHAPTER X.

DICK'S MISHAP.

MESSRS. Arithmetic and Mathematics were large manufacturers of ironware and machinery of every kind, of which they kept an immense assortment continually upon sale in a shop attached to the premises. They were said to be near connections as well as partners in business. Mr. Arithmetic had the name of a hard man, who looked sharply after every farthing, though not quite so hard perhaps as his partner Mr. Mathematics. And yet his workmen, who were all called ciphers, One, Two, Three, Four, Five, Six, Seven, Eight and Nine, never complained of their master. They said that they always received their just due, and as long as they kept in their own proper place, had never any reason to grumble.

Mr. Mathematics was a great philosopher, and shut himself up a good deal, that he might have leisure to invent new and curious machines. He did not show himself to customers so often as Mr. Arithmetic, who was the soul of the business, keeping all the workmen in order, scarcely ever out of his shop, and ready to serve all the world.

The Ironmongery establishment was on the top of a steep cliff that rose on the right side of the town of Education, just beyond Mr. Reading's large shop; and thither, on that fine summer's day, Dick and Pride wended their way.

"We must go up here," observed Dick, as they reached a narrow staircase cut in the cliff, and known by the name of the Multiplication stairs. I should not wonder if my readers had run up it many a time; if so, I need not tell them that it consists of twelve flights of steps, with twelve steps in every flight; that the first and second are so easy that a baby might almost toddle up them; that the two next are rather more steep, while the fifth is easier again; that the seventh and eighth are perhaps the worst; while the tenth flight quite tempts one to run, it is so delightfully smooth!

Dick was so active and vigorous a boy, that he mounted up to the top without even stopping to take breath. He had thence a fine view of the distant landscape; but what interested him most was to look down on the town which lay at his feet, and see the gilded names of the different Ologies shining on the fronts of their dwellings. There was Chemistry's beautiful shop too in view, with lovelycoloured glass jars in its windows; and Botany's vast garden not far off, bright with the hues of a thousand flowers. A fine place to look at, and a good place to dwell in, is this town of Education.

An immense building was now before Dick, though rather dull and unattractive in appearance; the names of Messrs. Arithmetic and Mathematics were in large black letters over the door. Dick entered, followed by Pride, and viewed with astonishment the vast variety of iron utensils around him. He could scarcely stop to look at the simple grates, called sums, which were the things that he came for, his eye was attracted by so many articles more curious and more interesting. There were big rules ofthree kettles, simple, inverse, and compound; reduction grindingmachines, and tables of weights of every species and size. There were innumerable instruments of various kinds that were known by the name of fractions; Dick did not exactly know their use, but they looked like instruments of torture. In an inner compartment of the place great machines were fizzing and whizzing, pistons rising and falling, wheels rolling and rumbling; that part belonged especially to Mr. Mathematics, and many of his partner's customers never entered that wing of the building.

"What do you require here?" said Mr. Arithmetic, a man dressed in irongray clothes, with a face which looked dry and hard as one of his own kettles, above which was a shock of irongray hair, which gave him rather a formidable appearance.

"I want to buy four little grates, to put in my house," said Dick, standing with his hand on his hip, and speaking in an easy tone, to show that he was not afraid of Mr. Arithmetic.

"I understand: my four first sumsAddition, Multiplication, Division, and Subtraction;" and the learned ironmonger pointed to a pile of some hundreds of the articles required by Dick.

"They are such simple, light little things," observed the boy, "that I'll carry off a couple with ease."

"As far as mere weight goes," said Pride, "you might bear away all four at once; but they are rather awkward to hold, and, if I understood you aright, you are obliged to carry all your purchases yourself."

"Ay," observed Mr. Arithmetic with a grim smile, "when the Prince of Wales himself came to shop in our town, he was obliged to be his own porter. Governesses and tutors may pack up the loads, but the pupils have the carrying after all."

"I certainly could manage two grates at once," observed Dick.

"I would advise you to be content with one at a time," said Arithmetic, "and come for the second tomorrow."

"Pick me out four good ones, not too small," cried Dick, trying to speak with an air of command; "I'll walk in further with my comrade, and have a look at yonder machines."

"Don't go too near those in work," said Mr. Arithmetic to Dick; "little boys may get into trouble if they meddle with things that they don't understand."

"Perhaps I can understand rather more than he supposes," muttered Dick, walking with head erect, and nose in the air, and a sort of swaggering step, which he probably thought best suited for a genius.

He passed on between rows of strange machines, whose use he could scarcely guess at; but he was ashamed to show any ignorance while Pride was close at his side. At last Dick stopped before a turninglathe, which had been made by a man called Euclid, and watched with interest and surprise all the curious articles called problems, which a clever workman was every few minutes forming with the circular saw.

"That does not look such hard work after all," said Dick; "the man has only to hold up the wood to that curious whirling machine, and it cuts it right into shape in a second. I think that I could do that myself."

"I should not advise you to try," said the workman, as he stopped his lathe for a short time, to go and look for a piece of hard wood. Pride glanced meaningly at Dick, and the boy's foot was in a minute on the board whose motion turned the circular saw.

"Give me that problem, I'll show you what I can do!" cried the eager Dick to his prompter; the next sound that he uttered was a yell, as the saw cut one of his fingers almost to the bone!

The cry drew Mr. Arithmetic to the spot. "Is the hand off?" was his cold hard question.

Poor Dick held up his bleeding finger.

"You've got your lesson cheaply," said the irongray man; "you had better know your own powers a little better before you meddle with matters like this. Wrap up your finger in your handkerchief, take up your grate, and be gone."

Much mortified by his morning's adventure, poor Dick in silence obeyed, not making an attempt to burden himself then with anything but a simple sum of Addition. It would have been well indeed for the boy if the experience of that day had cured him of his foolish presumption, and made him give up the company of Pride.

Back to contents

CHAPTER XI.

MISS FOLLY.

OH, dear! how frightful this great big dunce looks upon my wall!" cried poor Lubin; "and how shall I ever get rid of it? It's always staring me in the face, and telling tales of me to every one that comes into the room! What shall I do with the ugly thing?"

"Cover it over, dear Lubin," said Nelly, who felt for her brother's distress.

"Does it not look hideous?" cried Lubin, looking round with a woebegone face.

"It does look hideous indeed, and, if I were you, I would paper it over directly. No one could see it then."

"It's too high for me to reach," sighed Lubin.

"Yes, unless you were to use" Nelly hesitated, for she knew Lubin's dislike to the ladder of Spelling.

"I know what you mean," said Lubin gloomily; "but I won't use that ladder just now. Perhapsthere's no sayingperhaps some day I may learn to spell without stumbling, and get rid of that hateful word dunce."

"No time like the present," suggested little Nelly, with a smile.

"Not today, I say; I'm not in the humour; I've no fancy for a tumble on the floor."

"Have you a fancy, then, to go with me to Mr. Arithmetic's, to get grates for our little fireplaces?"

"That's where Dick cut his finger yesterday?"

"Yes; poor Dick!" exclaimed Nelly; "but we won't go so near to the machines."

"I'll keep at arms' length from all problems," cried Lubin. "Well, if you are going to the ironmonger's shop, we may just as well go together. Is Dick to be of the party?"

"No," replied Nelly; "yesterday's mishap had made him rather dislike Arithmetic, though the accident did not happen in his part of the building. But I hope that Matty will come; I was just going to invite her."

Casting one more vexed glance at the great dunce on his wall, Lubin sallied forth from his cottage with Nelly. As they crossed over the little green space to Matty's door, they heard such a jabber of voices within her cottage, that one might have thought that the little dwelling was full of chattering magpies.

In the parlour appeared Matty on her knees, examining with eager praises the contents of a large box of millinery open before her; while, talking so fast that she could hardly be understood, a curious creature stood beside her, whose dress, manner, and appearance, amazed both Lubin and Nelly.

The stranger was by nature very small and mean in appearance; but she had puffed out her dress with crinoline and hoops to a size so immense, that she half filled up Matty's little parlour, and it was hard to imagine how she had contrived to squeeze herself through the doorway. She had seven very full flounces, each of a different colour, adorned with flowers and beads. Her waist had been pulled in very tightly indeed, till it resembled that of a wasp; and a quantity of gaudy jewellery shone on her neck and arms. But the headdress of Miss Follyfor this was shewas still more peculiar than her figure. An immense plume of peacock's feathers stuck upright in her frizzled red hair, which was all drawn back from her forehead, to show as much as possible of her face. Her great goggle eyes were rolling about with a perpetual motion to match that of her tongue; and her cheeks, rouged till they looked like peonies, were dotted over with black bits of plaster. I don't know, dear reader, whether Miss Folly be an acquaintance of yours; if so, I hope that you will excuse my saying that, notwithstanding her rouge and her jewels, I consider her a perfect fright.

But here let us make no mistake. I know that there are certain persons who confuse between Miss Folly and Miss Fun, and fancy that these are names for one and the same person. I assure you that this is not the case; Folly and Fun are perfectly distinct. I own that laughing, singing, playful little Fun, is rather a pet of my own; she and I have had pleasant hours together; nay, I have actually consulted her when writing this very book. It is true that she needs to be kept in order, for her spirits get sometimes a little too wild; she must be forbidden to do any mischief, or give pain to any creature living. But when under good control, Fun is a bright and charming companion, especially to the young; and I delight in hearing her merry laugh, and in watching her sparkling eyes. But as for Folly, I cannot abide her; her mirth only makes me sad. Perhaps, before they lay down my book, my readers may more clearly distinguish what qualities make Miss Folly unlike that general favouriteFun.

Miss Folly went jabbering on: "Just try that bonnet on your head."
Page .
It was clear that Matty Desley was very well satisfied with her companion, and she turned over the wares with delight, as Miss Folly went jabbering on,

"There, now; that's something that I can quite recommend; it's decidedly à la mode, worn by all the duchesses, countesses, baronesses, and lady mayoresses, at all the balls, routs, conversaziones, and concerts given this season! Andyes, just try that bonnet on your head, and look at yourself in this glass"(Folly always carries a glass)"doesn't it show off the charming face?doesn't it suit the pretty complexion?doesn't it make you look quite bewitching, a lovely little fairy as you are?"

"Matty!" cried Lubin, the moment Folly paused to take breath, "we're going to Arithmetic the ironmonger; will you come with us and buy a new grate?"

"Multiplication is a vexation,
Addition is as bad;
The Rule of Three doth puzzle me,
And Fractions make me mad!"
cried Folly, rolling her goggle eyes, and thinking herself quite a wit.

"Was it not at Arithmetic's factory that Dick hurt himself yesterday?" said Matty.

"Hurt himself, did he?" interrupted Folly, who seemed resolved to take the largest share of the conversation. "Why did he not come to me for a salve? I've the best salve that ever was inventedFlattery salve, warranted to heal all manner of bruises and sores; yes, headaches, and heartaches, and all kinds of aches. It's patronized by all the heads of the nobility and gentry. I've tried it myself many a time, and always find it a perfect cure! When I've the highstrikes (I'm very subject to the highstrikes), I just rub a little on the tip of my ear, and it calms down my nerves like a charm. I wish you would try it!" she cried, turning to Lubin.

"I'm not subject to highstrikes, and don't want Flattery salve," said the boy, in his blunt, simple manner; "all I want is to know whether you, Matty, will go with us to the town of Education."

"I can't go today!" cried Matty, annoyed at being interrupted by her brother and sister; "I shall want every minute of Time's money to buy some of Miss Folly's pretty things!"

"Leave Miss Folly, I should say," cried Lubin, who had no want of plain commonsense; "a pleasant, goodhumoured smile makes a face look nicer than all that flummery there."

"Dear Matty, the days go fast," said Nelly, "and you know that our mother expects to find our cottages well furnished on her return. I really think that we've no Time money to spare upon what can be of no possible use."

"What would my Lady Fashion, my most particular friend, say if she could hear you?" exclaimed Folly, who had been struggling to get in a word, much talking being very characteristic of Folly; "sheLady Fashion I meanis always for the ornamental; the useful she leaves to the vulgar. As for your sister there" (Folly only condescended to speak to Matty), "she knows nothing, I see, of flounces, furbelows, fringes, and flowers; she'd put on a bonnet back part forward, or a shawl wrong side out; and she looks like a whippingpost, or a threadpaper, or a"

"Oh, stop that jabber, will you!" cried Lubin, putting his hands to his ears.

"Come with us, Matty," entreated Nelly, "and buy something solid and useful. Summer will soon be over, and when cold weather comes, what should we do without grates?"

"I can't come, and I won't come!" cried Matty pettishly; "don't you see that I'm exceedingly busy?"

"Come away, Nelly," said Lubin; "leave her to her fine Miss Folly; let her furnish her head, if she likes it, with fairies, furbelows, and flounces!"

Off went the brother and sister, but they had proceeded some way from the door before they got beyond reach of the sound of Miss Folly's chattering tongue.

Down hill Puzzle, across brook Bother, along Trouble lane, fat little Lubin and Nelly went very sociably together.

"I don't think that you're as lame as you were," said the boy.

"The way seems shorter than it did," observed Nelly; "but one feels the hill most when coming back."

As the children passed Mr. Reading's fine shop, little Alphabet peeped through the grating, to the no small annoyance of Lubin.

"Ha, ha! my brave fellow!" cried the dwarf, "have you mounted the ladder of Spelling, and have you now come to jump over my head?"

Lubin did not answer, but quickened his pace. He and his sister soon found themselves at the bottom of Multiplication stairs.

"I wonder how we shall ever get up to the top?" thought lame Nelly, as, with rather a disconsolate air, she glanced up the twelve flights of steps.

Back to contents

CHAPTER XII.

A VISIT TO ARITHMETIC.

IT'S a dreadful pull up this staircase!" exclaimed Lubin, as panting and puffing he stopped halfway, his fat round face flushed with fatigue till it looked almost the colour of a cock's comb.

"It is dreadfully tiring!" sighed Nelly, pausing a moment to take breath.

"It is worse than the ladder of Spelling!" cried Lubin. "I vote that we go back at once."

"Oh no, dear Lubin!" said his sister, immediately starting again on her weary ascent"perseverance, you know, conquers difficulties;" and as she uttered the words, the lame girl stumbled at that step seven times eight.

"You'll never succeed," observed Lubin.

"I'll try again," said the patient Nelly; and slowly but steadily she mounted.

Her example encouraged her brother to follow.

"I say, Nelly," observed Lubin, "what a plague all this education furnishing is! What lucky dogs those savages are who live in caves that want no fittings, and who have never heard of Reading papers, or ladders of Spelling, or this horrible Multiplication!"

Nelly could not help laughing.

"The very same thought was passing through my head," said she; "but I tried to drive it away, for it seemed to be only fit for Miss Folly."

"Perhaps a cave might not be so very pleasant," rejoined Lubin. "But I wish that some goodnatured fairy could furnish these cottages of ours with a stroke of her wand, and save us all this terrible trouble."

"It would not be so good for us, I daresay," said Nelly, stumbling again at nine times six.

"And why not?" inquired her brother.

"Why," replied Nelly, as she rubbed her bruised ankle, "I think that the trouble and pain serve to exercise our patience and perseverance, and to make us more fit to meet the trials which are sure to come when we are older. Besides," she added, still mounting as she spoke, "we take more pleasure in that which has cost us trouble than in that which we get with ease; and it is real enjoyment to feel that a difficulty has been overcome."

"I'm sure that we can have no pleasure from this Multiplication stair."

"Oh yes, when we get to the top!" cried Nelly, who had just reached the pleasant tenth flight, and now went along it hand in hand with her brother at a pace that was almost rapid.

"Hurrah! hurrah!" shouted Lubin, not long after, as he stood panting on the topmost step.

"Oh, what a charming view!" exclaimed Nelly. "I'm so glad that we persevered!"

"It's a tremendous big place, this town of Education," said Lubin, looking down from his height. "I don't like the look of all those Ologies. I'm afraid that a great lot of things are required for a really wellfurnished house."

"We have only to think of our grates at present," said Nelly. "Please keep close beside me, Lubin; for I've heard that Mr. Arithmetic is a terribly hard man, and I'm rather afraid to face him."

So again, hand in hand, the two children walked into the big shop together, and looked in wonder, as Dick had done, at the great heaps of goods within it.

"We won't go near that machinery part," whispered Lubin. "One of these big thundering engines would crack my poor head like a nutshell."

"What do you want?" asked the irongray man, coming from behind a great pile of coalscuttles.

Nelly squeezed Lubin's hand to make him speak first, for she was a shy little girl.

"We each want four sumgrates, for four little fireplaces," said Lubin"the very lightest that you can give us. I should like some no bigger than my shoe."

"You're made of different metal from the young fellow whom we had here yesterday," said Arithmetic, looking down with some scorn at the fat little boy. "You'll never cut your fingers by meddling with problems, I guess."

"You may answer for that," said Lubin.

Mr. Arithmetic, without further delay, produced specimens of his four simplest kinds of sum grates, like those from which Dick had been supplied. Lubin and Nelly soon chose Addition as their first purchase from Arithmetica grate so small and so light that even the little girl supported the burden with tolerable ease.

"You must come back tomorrow for something a little heavier," said Mr. Arithmetic. "Addition is simple enough; but Division needs a little greater effort of strength."

"We've done grand things today," exclaimed Lubin; "it's time enough to think about tomorrow."

"Oh, I will certainly come back then!" cried Nelly, not a little pleased at her present success.

Back to contents

CHAPTER XIII.

THE WONDERFUL BOY.

THAT evening Dick and his dark companion Pride sat in his cottage together. The boy looked out of spirits or out of temper. Perhaps his cut still pained him; perhaps the perpetual patter of the shower which was falling made him gloomy and dull, for a violent rain had come on, which continued during the whole of that night.

"Who would have thought," said Pride, "that lazy Lubin and lame Nelly would have mounted so bravely to the top of Multiplication staircase, and have carried back, safely over Bother, such nice little grates of Addition? You must really look sharp, Dick Desley, or they'll furnish their cottages before you."

"Before me!" exclaimed Dick, with a sneer. "I could do more with my little finger than Lubin with all his fat fist."

"Certainly," observed Pride, "it would be an intolerable disgrace to a clever fellow like you if you let any one get before you. You are not one who would endure to see another winning from you the crown of Success."

"I'll never see that," cried Dick, haughtily. "I should like to know who has a chance against me!"

"No one has the smallest chance against you, if you only exert yourself," said Pride. "If I were you I would put forth my powers, and do something to astonish them all."

"I will!" cried Dick, with decision. "I'll go to Arithmetic tomorrow, and bring back the three remaining sumgrates all at once. But what wretched weather we have this evening!" he exclaimed; "I'm afraid all the brightness of summer is going. And what's that on my wallthat dull stain as of damp, that seems creeping over my paper?"

"It is merely caused by the rain. I should think nothing of it," said Pride.

But Dick did think something of the stain. He saw that it marred the beauty of that upon which he had bestowed much diligent labour.

"I'll cross over to Nelly's cottage," he said, "and see if the damp is staining hers also."

Nelly was busy fixing in her grate. She looked upon her brother with a smile.

"How kind to come and see me through the rain!"

"I did not come to see you, but your paper. How is this?there is not a damp spot upon it!"

"Nor on Lubin's neither," remarked Nelly. "But I was with Matty just now, and the damp shows sadly on her fairies."

"What on earth can make the difference?" cried Dick.

"I do not know, unlessunless" Nelly hesitated before she added"unless it be that both Matty and you used the paste that Pride recommended."

"That has nothing to do with it," said Dick, as he quitted the cottage in displeasure.

But Nelly had been right in her guess. There will be an ugly stain upon any work which we only pursue with zeal because we want to outdo others in it.

Dick did not make his appearance on the following morning at the breakfasttable. The children still took their meals at the house Needful till their cottages should be better prepared.

"I am so glad that it has stopped raining," said Nelly, when she had finished her breakfast. "I have been wishing for the weather to clear, for I promised Mr. Arithmetic that I would go back for the grate of Division. Matty, dear, you will come with us today?"

Matty had come down to breakfast in a dress almost as ridiculously fine as that worn by Miss Folly herself. She tossed her head, and replied,

"I've something better to do than to buy, or carry, or scrub wretched sumgrates of Arithmetic. I'm going out with Miss Folly, to be introduced to some of her friends."

"But, Matty, the grates are quite necessary," urged Nelly. "We are soon to take up our quarters in our cottages, and sleep there as well as work. What shall we do when the cold weather comes if we've no means of having a fire?"

"How shall we cook our dinners?" asked Lubin. "If there's one thing more useful in a house than anything else, I should say it is a grate in the kitchen."

"Oh, Miss Folly tells me never to look forward to winter," cried Matty, "but just enjoy myself while I can. So I am not going to plague myself with either Addition or Division today. To look after such vulgar things is only a shopkeeper's business."

"But what will mother say," persisted Nelly, "if she find your cottage unfurnished?"

"Unfurnished, indeed!" cried Matty. "It will be far better furnished than yours. I mean to have French mirrors, and Italian paintings, and German glass and china. I shall get a tambourine also, and perhaps some day a guitar. Miss Folly tells me that Lady Fashion, her most particular friend, has all these; and though they make a fine show, they are not so dear as one would think."

"They are all good and beautiful things, I daresay," began Nelly; "but"

"But grates must come before mirrors, and carpets before German china," laughed Lubin. "We must buy what is needful first, and think of what is pretty afterwards."

"That may be your way; but it is not my way, and it was never the way of Miss Folly," cried Matty, as she flaunted out of the house.

"I wonder at Dick being so late," observed Nelly; "we ought to be off to the town."

"He is not late, but early," said Lubin. "He had had his breakfast, and started for the town of Education, before I was out of my bed."

"I wish that he had waited for us," cried Nelly; "it is so nice to go through our work all together. You and I had now better set off."

"I'm going presently," replied Lubin. "I've just five minutes to spare; and I'm about to step round to Amusement's bazaar, hard by here, to get a few barleysugar drops, to refresh me on my wearisome walk."

"I think that you had better delay your visit to the bazaar until you have done your business with Mr. Arithmetic. Our mother's proverb, you know, is, 'Duty first, and pleasure afterwards.' The sky is dark, the weather uncertain; we may be stopped from going altogether if we do not start off at once."

"I should like to be stopped altogether," said Lubin, with a smile. "I should not care if I never took another journey to the town of Education."

"What! after all that you said to Matty about the necessity of grates?"

"Ah, yes; they are needful enough, but they are not needed just at this moment. You may go on if you like it, I'll get my sugardrops first. Set off now, I'll soon overtake you; I won't spend much time at Amusement's."

Nelly sighed, but she saw that there was no use in further entreaty, so she set forth alone. The path down hill was slippery and wet from the rain that had fallen at nighta sister's kind word, or a brother's strong arm, would have been a real comfort now to the lame little girl. Often and often did Nelly turn and look behind her, to see if Lubin were not following after; but in vain she looked, not a sign appeared on the hill of the fat little sluggard.

Nelly came to the stream of Bother. The brook was muddy and swollen, and went racing on faster than usual. The steppingstones were scarcely seen above the brown waters that eddied around them.

"Oh dear, oh dear; I wish that Lubin or Dick were with me!" cried poor Nelly, as she gave one more anxious glance behind her. "It is miserable to have to go alone across such a stream as this." She put her little foot upon the first stone, she fancied that it trembled beneath her weightthen on the next, she was almost in the water. It was nothing but a strong sense of duty that made the poor child go on. With trembling steps and dizzy brain she proceeded on her dangerous way, and great was her relief when she reached in safety the farther shore.

"One difficulty is happily past, but how shall I enter the great town all alone? how shall I climb the wearisome stair? how shall I face cold stern Mr. Arithmetic, with no brother or sister to back me?" such were the reflections of Nelly as she made her way slowly along the muddy lane of Trouble. Some of my readers may have experienced what a dull and discouraging thing it is to do business all by one's self in the town of Education.

One difficulty, however, Nelly found less great than she had expected it to be. It is a curious fact, but well known to all, that those who have once mounted Multiplication staircase never complain any more of its steepness. Nelly ascended it without a single stumble, till, when she had almost reached the top, she met her brother Dick coming down from Mr. Arithmetic's. What was her astonishment to see the strong boy laden with three grates fastened together, Division, Subtraction, Multiplication, placed one on the top of another!

"O Dick, you can never carry all that at once!"

"I do carry all at once, as you may see," replied Dick, with a smile of triumph; "I'd advise you to get out of my way, lest I knock you over the staircase."

"Surely, surely you can't bear that great burden across the swollen brook, or up the steep hill."

"Take no fears for me: I can't fail with the crown of Success in my view!" exclaimed Dick, bearing his three grates aloft, as some warrior might carry his banner.

"If you would only wait a few minutes for me," began Nelly, but Dick at once cut her short.

"I wait for nobody!" he cried, pushing past his lame little sister. "If you had been up this morning as early as I was, you might have enjoyed the pleasure of my company." And so saying, Dick and his iron grates went clattering down the staircase.

Alone poor Nelly entered the shop, alone she took up her purchase, and alone she descended the twelve flights of steps, trembling under the weight of Division, which she had found a much more serious burden than little Addition had been.

"How could Dick carry three grates at a time," thought Nelly, "when one is almost more than I can support. But then I'm a poor, stupid, lame, little creature, and Dickoh, Dick is a wonderful boy!"

Back to contents

CHAPTER XIV.

THE THIEF OF TIME.

WHEN Lubin had said that he would not spend much Time money at Amusement bazaar, he had fully intended to keep his word. He meant to go steadily on his walk to Education, or, as we might call it, "do his lessons," so soon as he had had a little diversion. But let me advise all my dear young readers to put off their visits to Mrs. Amusement's till they have spent such hours as business requires in the town of Education. Let them count their money before they set out, spend a good portion of it wisely and well, and then, with light hearts and easy consciences, they may go to refresh and enjoy themselves at Mrs. Amusement's bazaar.

Which of us does not know that bazaar? It lies on the further side of hill Puzzle, very near to the cottages of Head, and a beautiful large cherrytree hangs its branches over the door. The house is not lofty, but low and wide, with a multitude of bright little windows. It is divided within into numerous stalls, each possessing separate attractions. There is one much frequented by boys, where bats and balls, bows and arrows, models of boats, and little brass guns are seen in great profusion. At another stall there are pretty dolls of every size and shape, wooden, wax, and guttapercha; some made to open and shut their eyes, and some to utter a sound. There are few prettier sights than that of a number of rosy, goodhumoured children, who have finished their lessons well, and are going, each with a bright hour or two in his hand, to the bazaar of Mrs. Amusement.

The stall that most attracted fat Lubin was one at which sweetmeats were sold: raspberry, strawberry, pineapple drops, bull'seye, pink rock, and chocolate sticks, barleysugar twisted into shapes more various than I can describe or remember. Lubin had taken his five minutes in his hand, and now spent them easily enough; but there were more, oh, many more things that he thought that he would like from the stall. He went humming on as he examined the sweetmeats a favourite proverb of his, "All work and no play makes Jack a dull boy." But the fat little dunce might have added, "All play and no work will make Lubin a duller."

Full of interest in all that he saw, with his eyes greedily fixed on the stall, Lubin did not notice a lean, small figure, which, softly as a serpent on the grass, had stolen up to his side. This was no other than Procrastination, a pickpocket well known to the police, who had often been caught in the very act of robbing her Majesty's subjects of Time, had been tried and sent to prison, but on getting out had always returned to his bad occupation again. The poet Young long ago set up a placard to warn men to take care of their pockets, giving notice to all concerned that "Procrastination is the thief of Time;"

but, in spite of this warning, there are few amongst us who must not own with regret that the stealthy hand of Procrastination has robbed us of many an hour.

Have you never suffered from Procrastination, good reader? It is he who makes us put off till tomorrow what ought to be done today. It is he who whispers, "It will be time enough," when a duty should be performed directly. If you are aware, at this very moment, while you sit with this book in your hand, that you ought to be busy with Arithmetic, or should write a letter to a friend, or do some little piece of business, start up without an instant's delay, shut this book with a clap; perhaps you may then catch between its leaves the sly fingers of thief Procrastination.

Poor Lubin was not on his guard: he noticed not the form that crept after him as noiselessly as a shadow. Procrastination took the opportunity when the boy's attention was most engaged with the sweetmeats, to draw out Time's fairy purse, and rifle it of its precious contents. Silently then he replaced the purse emptied for that day, in hopes, perhaps, that when the morrow filled it with new hours and minutes, he might rob its possessor again of the treasure which he guarded so badly.

"Well, now," exclaimed Lubin, "I can't stop much longer, for I promised Nelly to follow her quickly, and I know that I ought to be at Mr. Arithmetic's by this time. I'll just spend two or three minutes more on those sugarplums shaped like marbles, and then away to my business and work like a man."

So Lubin plunged his fat hand into his pocket, and drew forth his purse of Time. In went his fingers, fumbling about to pull out the minutes that he wanted, but he fumbled and felt in vainnot an hour was leftnot a single little minute, to pay for what he required.

"It's that rogue Procrastination who has robbed me!" exclaimed the indignant boy, as turning sharply round he caught a glimpse of a slim little figure sneaking round the corner of a counter.

Lubin instantly gave chase. Fat as he was, it was wonderful to see how he dodged the pickpocket, first round this stall, then round that, shouting all the time, "Stop, thief! stop, thief!" as loudly as he could bawl. I need scarcely add that all the boy's efforts were useless. Who ever yet recovered lost Time? Out of breath and out of heart, poor Lubin stopped panting at last; Procrastination had had a fair start, and carried off his spoil in triumph.

"There's no use in attempting to go to Education today, I've not a minute left," was Lubin's sorrowful reflection. "Oh, that I had started with my sister, had thought of my business before my play, what useful things I might then have bought with the hours which are now lost to me for ever!"

Back to contents

CHAPTER XV.

DUTY AND AFFECTION.

IN the meantime, poor Nelly had been wearily wending her way along the lane of Trouble, with her burdensome Division on her shoulder. She felt, as many a little student has felt, quite out of humour for work; her arms ached, and so did her head; the mud in the lane was so deep that she could scarcely keep on her shoes, and she sometimes sank in it almost up to her ankle.

Thus in sorrowful plight the lame girl at last reached the brook of Bother. Its brown turbid waters looked rougher and deeper and dirtier than they ever had done before. The steppingstones had almost disappeared!

Nelly Desley heaved a long weary sigh as she looked before her, and rubbed her forehead very hard, as puzzled children are wont to do.

"Oh, this tiresome Division, how shall I ever manage it! I never saw Bother so bad. Nine's in fiftynine"another violent rub; "I know what will be in, a poor little girl will be in brook Bother!and what's to be carried? why this grate is to be carried, and a very great vexation it is."

Weary Nelly sat down, almost in despair, on a stone by the bank of the stream. What object attracted her eye, some yards lower down the current of the brook, round which the muddy waves were eddying and rolling?

"Whycan it be?yes, there are Dick's three grates all together, Division, Multiplication, and Subtraction!" Nelly started up in alarm: "Oh, what can have become of my brother?"

A little reflection soon reassured Nelly. Dick, the most active of boys, and a famous swimmer besides, could not have come to much harm in a brook in which, though many have been ducked, no one has ever yet been quite drowned. It seemed clear that the boy had found the weight which, prompted by Pride, he had tried to carry, somewhat too much for his strength; and, being unable to carry it across the waters of Bother, had flung down his tiresome burden, which, by the force of its own weight, had stuck fast in the mud of the brook.

"Well, if Dick has failed, I need not mind failing," cried Nelly. "I think that I'll do what he has done, and fling away this horrid Division,oh, what a relief that would be! But still, would it not be foolishwould it not be wrongto give way so to impatience? My dear mother bade me obey Mr. Learning for her sake, she wishes my cottage to be properly furnished; I must not be a sluggard or a coward. I must do my best to get over this Bother."

"Well resolvedbravely resolved," said a voice on the other side of the brook; and from behind the clump of willows which drooped their long branches in the stream, Nelly saw two beautiful maidens come forth. They were like, and yet unlike, each other. Both were very fair to look on, both of noble height and graceful mien; but the one had an air of more stately dignity, such as might beseem a queen; and her large dark eyes looked graver and more thoughtful than those of her sister. The other had smiling soft blue eyes, beaming with tender love, and the sunlight fell on her golden hair till it seemed like a glory around her.

These lovely maidens were no strangers to Nelly, almost from her infancy she had looked upon them as friends; many sweet counsels and good gifts had the lame little girl received from Duty and Affection.

"Oh, Duty!" exclaimed Nelly, who was rejoiced to find herself no longer alone, "only show me how I can get across, and I will not mind labour or trouble."

Duty retired for a few moments to her retreat behind the willows, and then returned, bearing on her shoulder a narrow plank. With the help of smiling Affection she placed this across the stream.

"This plank, dear child," said calm, stately Duty, "was cut from the tree of Patience, and small as it seems, can well support your weight. Boldly venture upon it; the stream runs fast today, you are no longer able to ford it, but on the plank of Patience you safely can pass across."

Giddy and tired as she felt, Nelly instantly obeyed the voice of Duty, and placed her foot on the plank. Duty leant forward, and held out her firm hand to aid her, and soon the trembling child and her wearisome burden were safe on the bank nearest to the cottages of Head.

"Oh, I am so glad to be well over!" exclaimed Nelly, and with exceeding pleasure she looked up in the face of Duty, and smiled.

"And now sit down and rest yourself, dear one," said Affection, spreading a thick mantle on the grass, that its dampness might not hurt the child.

"May I?" asked Nelly timidly of Duty.

The beauteous maiden bowed her head in assent. There was no sternness now in her look; Duty is no enemy to innocent enjoymentrather should we say that there is no real enjoyment but that which is found by those who take Duty for their guide and their friend.

"See, here is refreshment for you," said Affection, placing before the wearied child a rich cluster of delicious fruit. How sweet is such refreshment given by the hand of Affection, how doubly sweet after efforts made at the call of Duty!

Never, perhaps, had Nelly Desley passed a happier hour than she did now on the bank of that stream which she had crossed with such trouble and fear. She now looked with pleasure at the waves as they rushed so rapidly by her.

One thought only disturbed little Nelly. "Poor Dick! I wish that I knew of his safety," said she.

"He is safe enough," replied Duty; "but there, as you may see, lie his three grates in the mud of the stream."

"If he had only had the plank of Patience," exclaimed Nelly.

"It was offered to him as well as to you," said Duty with a graver air; "and I thought at first that your brother would have gladly accepted my offer. But there came to this shore of the brook a dark, illfavoured lad"

"It must have been Pride!" exclaimed Nelly, who knew too well her brother's companion.

"This Pride," continued Duty, "began to taunt and to scoff. 'Holloa!' he shouted across the stream, 'will a genius like you stoop to be directed by a woman! Duty is for slaves, and Patience for donkeys. Kick aside that miserable plank, and clear the brook with a bound, as you've often cleared it before.'"

"Dick is a wonderful boy for jumping," cried Nelly, who greatly admired her brother.

"He jumped once too often," observed Duty; "this time he jumped not over but into the brook, and mighty was the splash which he made!"

Even gentle Affection could scarcely help laughing at the recollection of the scene.

"But he scrambled out!" exclaimed Nelly.

"Yes; very muddy, and wet, and cross, leaving all his three grates behind him. I do not know whether Pride dried Dick's clothes, and wiped off the mud, they both ran off as fast as they could; I think that your brother was ashamed to be seen, after having so scornfully refused the aid of Affection and Duty."

It was now time for Nelly to continue her walk and return to her own little cottage. Her beautiful friends accompanied her all the way up hill Puzzle, and made the steep way quite pleasant by their cheerful, wise conversation. Tiring as her lonely expedition to the town of Education had been, Nelly never in future times remembered without a feeling of enjoyment her little adventure by the brook where she had met with Duty and Affection.

Dick with some trouble recovered his grates from the stream. But he never looked at them with pleasure, for they served to remind him of the day when, prompted by foolish Pride, he had overtasked his powers, and, spurning the plank of Patience, had gone floundering into brook Bother!

Back to contents

CHAPTER XVI.

GRAMMAR'S BAZAAR.

I CAN NOT undertake to describe all the expeditions to Education, nor the various purchases made by the children; but I will here mention the first visit made by the Desleys to Grammar's famous bazaar, a place much frequented by all those who dwell in the town.

I need hardly tell my readers that Grammar's Bazaar lies in quite an opposite direction from Mrs. Amusement's, and that the two concerns have no connection whatever with each other. There are no sweetmeats sold in the former; the goods are all called words, and are arranged in perfect order on nine stalls, kept by nine sisters, well known by the name of Parts of Speech. These sisters live and work together in the greatest harmony and comfort, and are highly respected by all the inhabitants of the town of Education. Some indeed call them "slow" and "tiresome," and Miss Folly has been heard to declare that the very mention of them gives her the fidgets; but neither you nor I, dear reader, form our opinions by those of Miss Folly.

It was on a fine morning in summer that Dick, Lubin, Matty, and Nelly paid their first visit to Grammar's Bazaar. They entered it by a low porch, half choked up with parcels of words tied up in sentences ready to be sent to various customers.

"A dull, dark place this is!" exclaimed Lubin; "I would not give Amusement's Bazaar for fifty like this."

"Any chance of having one's pocket picked here?" said Dick, with a malicious wink at his brother.

"Let's visit all the stalls one after another," cried Matty, "before we make any purchase; I like to see all that's to be seen. What a comical little body is standing behind the first counter; she is not as big as Alphabet, I should say."

"She looks like his sister," observed Nelly; "but I suppose that she is one of the Parts of Speech." And she read the name "Article" fastened up at the back of the stall.

"What may you sell here, my little lady?" asked Dick, in his easy, selfconfident way; "I see only three hooks on your counter."

Miss Article Part of Speech had to stand upon a stool that her head might peep over the top of her stall. "I'm but a little creature," said she, with a goodhumoured smile; "a, an, and the are all the words that I'm trusted to sell. If you want to see a larger assortment, pass on to my sister Noun; she has many thousands of words to show you, models of everything that can be seen, heard, or felt in the world."

Surely enough a most prodigious collection appeared on the counter of Noun, a large portly maiden who presided over the stall next to that of Article. There were cups and saucers, pins and needles, caps and bonnets, models of houses, churches, beasts, birds, and fishes, by far too numerous to describe.

"These are all common," observed Noun, seeing the eyes of Dick fixed admiringly upon the collection; "I have behind me some more curious things that have all names of their own," and she pointed to a row of small figures. "These are not common but, proper," she continued; "you will notice here Wellington, Napoleon, Nelson, and our gracious sovereign Victoria."

Dick, Lubin, Matty, and Nelly paying their first visit to Grammar's Bazaar.
Page .
"And oh, look here, at Miss Adjective's counter!" cried Matty; "she keeps such a lot of dolls' things to dress up the figures of Noun. A pretty, nice, curious cape"

"An absurd, ridiculous, preposterous cap," added Dick.

"Observe," said Adjective with a courteous air, "that I arrange my words in three rows, one above another, which I call degrees of comparisonpositive, comparative, superlative."

"I see, I see," exclaimed Dick; "here's a bonnet, frightfulthat's positive; another more frightfulthat's comparative; and this with the superlative yellow tuft, I should call the most frightful of all. So, Nelly's cleverthat's positive"

"I don't think so," murmured Nelly.

"Matty's clevererthat's comparative."

Matty laughed.

"And I am superlatively cleverwithout doubt the cleverest of all!"

"In your own opinion," growled Lubin.

Nelly wandered on to the next stall, which was kept by the maiden Pronoun. Though smaller in size, she was so much like her sister Noun as to be frequently taken for her. As it was a trouble to stout Noun to go far or move fast, she very often sent Pronoun upon various errands in her stead. Pronoun sold not many words; such as she had were mere pictures of such as were kept by her sister. I, thou, he, she, and it, and some others which we need not stop to enumerate.

"Here's a famous big stall!" exclaimed Dick, stopping in front of Verb's, which was a very remarkable one, being covered with clockwork figures all in motion. One could see by them what it is to plough, to sow, to reap, to work, to weep, and to dance. The counter of Verb was almost as extensive as that of her sister Noun.

"How do you make all these things move?" said Dick with some curiosity to Verb.

"I conjugate them; that is, wind them up," she replied, showing a small brass key.

"Is it easy to conjugate them?" asked the boy.

"Easy enough with the regular words," replied Verb, "but a good many of mine are quite irregular in their construction, and it is hard to conjugate them."

"And if one conjugate them carelessly, I suppose," said Dick, "that there would be a great crack or whiz, and the whole affair would go to smash."

"Oh, don't stop there asking such questions!" cried Lubin; "I'm heartily tired of this stupid bazaarand if you go on so slowly, we shall never get to the end!"

"I like to understand things," said Dick; "there's a great deal to attract one's attention in this curious counter of Verb."

"Adverb, who keeps the next one," observed Nelly, "sells stands for her sister Verb's figures, to display them nicely, prettily, safely!"

"Badly, crookedly, awkwardly!" cried Dick, who was in one of his funny moods. "I don't like the look of Adverb, I think that she's given to lies!"

"The three sisters who have the last stall," whispered Matty to Dick, "seem all but poor little creatures!"

"I should call them small, smaller, and smallest, like the three degrees of comparison," laughed Dick, "but I see their names at the backs of their counters,Preposition, Conjunction, Interjection."

"Pray, Miss Preposition, what are these?" asked Nelly, as she took up some small labels from that lady's stall, with from, by, of, and such names upon them.

"They are to show in what case Noun's words are to be packed," replied Preposition politely. "You may remark yonder boxes with Nominative, Possessive, and such names painted upon them; it is my business to label my sister's goods, that they may be packed according to rule."

"It must be stupid work to deal in nothing but tickets!" exclaimed Dick; "if I were a Part of Speech, I'd be Noun rather than Preposition! And what has Conjunction to sell?"

"Only little balls of string to tie bundles of words together, such as and, either, or; and scissors to divide the bundles, such as neither, nor, notwithstanding."

"Oh, come here, come here!" cried Matty eagerly; "there's nothing amusing to look at on the counters of Conjunction or Preposition, but Interjection has something very funny! Look at these guttapercha balls shaped like faces, some showing pleasuresome horrorsome surprise; just give them a little squeeze, and hear how you make them squeak!"

Lubin pressed one of the heads between his fat fingers, and oh! ah! squeaked the red lips.

"I'll try one!" cried Dick, catching up another; "it's so like Matty's friend, Miss Folly, that I'm sure that she sat for her likeness!" He thumped it down on the counter, and out came a shrill "lackaday!"

"I think," laughed Nelly, "that Interjection sells the funniest words of all!"

"And the ones that we could best do without," said Dick scornfully, throwing down the lackaday ball.

The children did not leave the Grammar Bazaar emptyhanded. I must just remark that Matty loaded herself most with words from the stall of Adjective, choosing most of them from the Superlative row; and that Lubin, notwithstanding the neat labels of Miss Preposition, never knew how to put one of the words which he got from Noun or Pronoun into its own proper case.

CHAPTER XVII.

PRIDE AND FOLLY.

ONE day Mr. Learning, having finished a whole volume of travels for breakfast, made up his mind to pay a visit to his charges at the cottages of Head. He walked, as usual, at a rapid pace, with long strides, looking neither to the right hand nor to the left; his thoughts too busy with researches into the manners and peculiarities of distant lands, for him to notice how autumnal hues were already tinging the trees, or how summer roses were giving place to the convolvulus and the dahlia. Mr. Learning did not go emptyhanded; he carried with him as presents to the young Desleys four small hammers of Memory, and four bags of brass nails called Dates.

This time the first cottage which he entered was that of Dick, and he would doubtless have been pleased to see the numerous articles for ornament and use with which it already was furnished, had not the first object which met his eye been the ugly figure of Pride.

Pride was engaged in making a list of all the furniture in Dick's dwelling, very much like an auctioneer's puff. Everything, according to him, was "firstrate," "of superior quality," or, "fit for the residence of any nobleman in the land." Pride sat with his back to the door, and therefore was not aware of the entrance of Learning, till the stately gentleman in spectacles tapped him on the shoulder with one of the hammers.

Up jumped Pride in a moment. He had no time to hide himself, or to beat a retreat, so, being one of the most impudent fellows in the world, he resolved to brave out the matter with the solemn philosopher.

"I did not expect to find you here again," said Mr. Learning in his stiffest and coldest manner.

"Well, I'm surprised to hear that," replied saucy Pride, resting his hand on his hip, and trying to look quite at his ease; "as I go everywhere, and am welcomed by everybody, it's natural enough that I should chance to meet the most potent, grave, and reverend Mr. Learning."

"Where is your master?" asked Learning shortly.

"My master, indeed!" echoed Pride; "Dick never yet mastered me. I should rather say that I am his master!"

"Where has he gone?" inquired Learning, without seeming to notice the insolent remark.

"He has gone to History's shop, to purchase a carpet for his parlour. He is sure to select a pattern of the newest and most elegant design."

"Then I leave these for him," said the grave philosopher; "a bag full of bright brass Dates, and a hammer of Memory to knock them well in."

"If you had brought a sackful instead of a bagful," observed Pride, "it would not have been too much for Dick Desley; and as for the hammerdon't you know that he has a prodigiously fine Memory of his own?"

Without condescending to reply, Mr. Learning put down his gifts, turned round, and, quitting the cottage which harboured so impudent a guest, went to the next one, which was Lubin's. The door, as usual, was wide open, and the place deserted and empty. Mr. Learning did not even cross the threshold, so disgusted was he at the unfurnished, untidy state of the sluggard's home.

"I may as well leave these for him, but he'll never know how to use them," muttered Learning, throwing in the hammer and nails.

He then crossed over to Matty's pretty cottage. Her door was also ajar, and grave Mr. Learning stopped at it for some moments in astonishment at the sight which presented itself to his view.

Miss Folly, in her seven flounces, her beads and flowers, peacock's plume, rouge, ribbons, and all, was half reclining on the uncarpeted floor, engaged in blowing bubbles. As each rose from the bowl of her pipe, swelling and shining, and then mounting aloft, she watched it with a look of affected delight and admiration in her upturned eyes. No contrast could be imagined greater than that between the stately gentleman clothed in black, with his broad intellectual brow, spectacled eyes, and grave, solemn manner; and light, fantastical, frivolous Miss Folly, clad in the most absurd of styles, but looking as though she thought herself the very pink of perfection.

"Dear, who can that funny old fogie be!" exclaimed Folly, as she caught sight of grave Mr. Learning.

"Who may you be, and what are you doing?" asked Learning, with less politeness than he usually showed to ladies.

"You don't mean to say that you've never heard of me!" cried Folly, her words bubbling out fast like water out of a bottle; "you must be Mr. Ignorance, if you don't know that I'm Mademoiselle Folly, the most particular friend of lovely Lady Fashion, and the inventress of tightlacing, steelhoops, hairpowder, masks, periwigs"

"Flattened heads, blackened teeth, noserings, liprings, and tattooing," added Mr. Learning, remembering the account of a tribe of savages which he had been reading that morning.

"And as to what I am doing," continued Miss Folly, taking up her pipe, which she had laid down on the entrance of a stranger, "I'm very usefully employed: I'm furnishing the cottage of Miss Matty Desley."

"Furnishing!" exclaimed Mr. Learning in surprise, as Miss Folly, with distended cheeks, commenced blowing another bubble.

Folly was too busy at that moment to reply, even her tongue for a while was silent; but after she had succeeded in filling a big bubble, and had loosened it from the pipe with a gentle shake, she vouchsafed a little explanation.

"Yes, I'm furnishing the cottage with fancies; their poetical name is daydreams, cheap, elegant bubblefancies."

"You must take me for an idiot!" exclaimed Mr. Learning; "no one in his senses could ever dream of furnishing a house with bubbles!"

Miss Folly was so intently gazing after the ascending bubble that she seemed to forget even the presence of the sage. As the airy globule ascended, she began pouring forth a stream of disconnected nonsense, seeming to speak merely for her own pleasure, as her words could certainly not be intended for the information of any listener.

"A carriage and foursleek bays with long tails; no, white horses with pretty pink rosettes, and harness all glittering with silver! Drive through Londonup and down Hyde Parktaken for the Queenbowingsmilingah me, the bubble has burst!"

"This is some poor creature that has lost her wits!" thought the astonished Mr. Learning, scarcely knowing whether to regard Miss Folly with pity or with contempt. Already another bubble was swelling on the bowl of her pipe, and in a minute another bright ball was floating aloft in the air.

"Exquisite beautygreat attractionssuch a voicesuch a mannersuch a killing smile! An ode from the poetlaureate; bouquets, sent without end; roses in the middle of winter; a hundred and fifty scented pink notes on Valentine's day; the star of the season; thelackaday! that lovely bubble has gone for ever!"

"It's time that I should go too," said Mr. Learning; "I've heard enough of nonsense to last for a lifetime!"

He was about to depart when Matty suddenly burst into the cottage, in her eager haste almost knocking down her astonished guardian with a roll of goods which she carried on her shoulder. The shock of the collision was great, but not so great as the shock to poor Matty at so suddenly coming upon Mr. Learning when she only expected to find Miss Folly. She dropped her burden with an exclamation of surprise, and then tried to stammer forth an apology, but knew not how to begin. Mr. Learning stood straight before her, more erect and stately than ever, sternly looking down through his steel spectacles at the confused and blushing girl. Miss Folly, however, was quite at her ease, and hastily pushing aside her basin and pipe, began instantly to unroll the large parcel which Matty had dropped in her fright.

"Ah, I knew it would be so! You have chosen the sweetest patternthe prettiestmost tastefulmost charming little carpet that ever a girl set eyes on!" and she began spreading out on the floor a fabric so thin, that it seemed as if made of roseleaves.

"Did you buy that trash from Mr. History?" said Mr. Learning sternly to Matty.

"NowhyI ownMiss Folly recommended me rather to try Mr. Fiction, who lives close to Amusement's bazaar. It is a great matter, you know, not to have to cross over brook Bother, or carry a carpet uphill. And Mr. Fiction has such a magnificent shop, and his wares are so very cheap."

"Cheap and often worthless!" exclaimed the angry guardian, striking the carpet with his heel, and proving the truth of his words by tearing a great hole in the middle. "I brought a gift for you, Matilda Desley, but I have no intention of leaving it here now. My hammer of Memory, my bright brass Dates, are not required to fasten down such miserable trash as this! But," he muttered as he strode away, "it is at any rate all of a piece! a carpet framed by Fiction is just the thing for a cottage papered with fairies, furnished with fancies, and occupied by Miss Folly!"

"Ha, ha, ha!" laughed Folly, the moment that his back was turned, "I'm glad that the old owl has flown offhe looked ready to peck out my eyes!"

I should like, with wise Mr. Learning, to bid farewell to Folly for ever. Perhaps my readers may wonder that I should have introduced them to a creature so very absurd. I should not have done so had I had no suspicion that Folly might intrude herself, without introduction, when they themselves are furnishing their own little cottages of Head. Has no little girl who now gazes on this page, ever sat for hours blowing bubbles of fancies with Folly, listening to worsemore ridiculous nonsense than that which shocked Mr. Learning? Has she not delighted to imagine herself great, rich, beautiful, and admired? has she not consulted Folly about her dressspent her precious minutes and hours on a lookingglassor a fanciful garment, or a worthless work of Fiction, when duties had to be performed, when valuable things were to be bought in the good town of Education?

Ah, dear little laughing reader, have I, like grave Mr. Learning, caught some one in the very fact of harbouring Miss Folly? Turn her outat once turn her out! She is a silly companion, an unsafe guide; she will never make you loved, respected, or happy. Though not quite so dark and dangerous as Pride, she is much more closely related to him than people would at first imagine; there is much of Pride in Follyand oh, for poor, weak, ignorant beings like ourselves, is not Folly seen in all Pride!

Back to contents

CHAPTER XVIII.

THE CARPET OF HISTORY.

MR. LEARNING now stood at the top of hill Puzzle, watching Dick, Lubin, and Nelly, returning laden with carpets from History's shop. Though the carpets, like the rooms, were but small, they were rather heavy burdens for children in wet and slippery weather.

Learning smiled his own quiet smile, to see the different and characteristic movements of his young charges, the Desleys. Dick, the quick and energetic Dick, was halfway up hill Puzzle when his brother and sister were only beginning to ascend. His bright young face was flushed, but rather with pleasure than fatigue; he sped on with a light elastic tread, neither panting nor pausing, but bearing the carpet of History as though he felt not its weight. He moved all the more swiftly for seeing that his guardian's eye was upon him, and on reaching the crown of the hill, saluted Mr. Learning with a very selfsatisfied air.

"You make good progress," observed the sage, politely returning his salute.

"Oh, I get over everything with a hop, skip, and jump," replied the laughing boy, forgetting his flounder in Bother, "and you'll soon have the pleasure of presenting me with the silver crown of Success. It's nearly time, I should think, for you to introduce me to all your learned friends the Ologies! But there's one gentleman in Education whom I fancy more than allthe glorious old fellow who keeps a shop filled with jars of different colours, retorts, electricmachines, and bottles of powders and gases; I've heard that he sells such fireworks as would set all the world in a blaze!"

"You mean, of course, Mr. Chemistry," replied the sage; "he is my much valued friend; there is not a more pleasing companion to be found in the whole town of Education than he. But you are yet far too young, Master Dick, to make the acquaintance of so superior and intellectual a man. His goods are not yet for you, though in time you may make them your own. Attend at present to your carpets and your grates; furnish your cottage with facts from General Knowledge; a day perhaps may arrive when you will be ready for things more abstruse, and then I'll introduce you myself both to the Ologies and to Mr. Chemistry, which latter will, I have no doubt, display to you all his magazine of wonders."

"Always putting off!" muttered Dick between his teeth; "always treating one like a mere child. I shall have long enough to wait if I wait for the introduction of slow Mr. Learning. I can do very well without it, and shall certainly try some day whether, by putting a bold face on the matter, I am not able to make my own way to the favour of Mr. Chemistry!"

These last words were only overheard by Pride, for Dick had already entered his cottage. In a few minutes more the sound of his busy hammer told that he was already setting vigorously to work to nail down his History carpet.

"How comparatively slowly the two other children make their way up the hill!" said Learning, who stood watching Lubin and Nelly. "Why, the boy has twice sat down to rest on his bundle; and now, surely my spectacles must be at fault, can he be rolling his carpet up the hill, instead of carrying it on his shoulder! In a fine miry state it will be by the time that he reaches his dwelling!"

Surely enough the lazy boy was getting on with his History carpet in the laziest of ways, pushing instead of bearing, rolling it along as if it were a snowball, and seeming to be quite regardless of the fact that the path was covered with mud! Have none of my readers done the same, been content to get up a task in any way, however slothful and careless?

"Are you not ashamed of that?" exclaimed Mr. Learning, pointing to the dirty roll of carpet, as Lubin gained the top of the hill.

"Oh, sir, the mud will rub off when it is dry," said the boy with an air of unconcern; "the inner side, where the pattern is, cannot be soiled in the least."

"Unroll it and see," said stern Mr. Learning.

Lubin slowly obeyed, and had certainly little cause to be pleased with the condition of his new purchase. The pattern, which was full and rich, represented a hundred different scenes of interest. There was the wooden horse of old Troy; here appeared the gallant sons of Sparta defending the pass of Thermopylæ; great men of Greece and of Rome, British monarchs and statesmen in varied costumes and different attitudes, adorned the History carpet. Adorned, did I say? rather once had adorned, for all was now a jumble of confusion! There was a great blot of mud just over the face of Julius Cæsar, and not a single Roman emperor stood out clear and distinct. In silent indignation Mr. Learning turned away, leaving Lubin to do the best that he could with his poor soiled History carpet.

Nelly Desley, weary, but cheerful, had just carried her burden home. She was unrolling it now in her simple but beautifully neat little parlour, and surveying with great delight the charming pattern upon it.

"Of all the purchases that I have made, this pleases me most!" she cried. "What a wonderful variety of pictures, so amusing and interesting! Ah, there is good Queen Philippa on her knees, begging for the citizens of Calais; and there brave Joan of Arc leading on her soldiers to battle! And there, oh, there are the holy martyrs tied to the stake for the sake of the truth, looking so calmly and meekly upwards, as though they had no fear of dying! I can never pass a dull evening now with this wonderful carpet before me; it seems as though it would take a lifetime to know all its various scenes."

"Yes," said Mr. Learning, who had entered her parlour unobserved, "that beautiful carpet will serve as a constant feast for the mind. Fiction may boast that his dyes are the brightest; this I utterly deny; no colours are so vivid or so lasting as those that have been fixed by Truth, and these should alone be employed in the carpets which History produces."

Mr. Learning then graciously bestowed upon Nelly the gift of the hammer and nails, and quitted the cottages of Head well satisfied with at least one of his charges.

Back to contents

CHAPTER XIX.

HAMMERING IN DATES.

KNOCKknockknock! "Oh, this wearisome hammering!" sighed poor Nelly, as stooping over her carpet till the blood swelled the veins of her forehead, she tried to fasten in, one by one, the datenails which Mr. Learning had given. "I do not see why it is needful to knock in all these tiresome nails! Lubin has thrown his whole stock into a rubbish corner, I know, and says that he never means to prick his fingers again by thrusting them into such a bag!" knockknock! "Stephen came to the throne in , or , I'm sure I don't know whichand, what's more, I don't care! Ah!" the last exclamation was a cry of pain, for the hammer in the girl's awkward hand had come down with some force on her fingers.

"Well, Nelly, what is the matter?" asked Lubin, showing his jolly fat face at the door.

"I'm tired to death of these dates!" replied Nelly, raising her flushed face at the question.

"So was I with the very first of them; I never got beyond William the Conqueror; my carpet will stick on very well without nails, if no one takes to dancing a jig upon it! You are just wearing your spirits out, Nelly, and I'm sure that I wouldn't do that for any man, least of all for that sour Mr. Learning, who scribbled Dunce on my wall!"

"I think," said Nelly, "that my friend Duty would tell me to go hammering on with these dates."

"Duty would keep one in tight order," laughed Lubin, "but I prefer following my own pleasure. I'm off to Amusement's bazaar, and I advise you to come with me now."

"Oh, Lubin, not now; not till I have finished my work."

"Then I'll go without you," said the boy, leaving poor Nelly to her troublesome task.

Scarcely had Nelly begun her hammering again, when Matty popped in her pretty little face.

"Why, Nelly, what's the use of tiring yourself like that! You will never manage to knock in all those nails!"

"I am afraid that I will not," sighed poor Nelly.

"Do as I do," continued Matty. "Miss Folly, kind creature, has supplied me with spangles, which are, all the world must own, just as pretty as any brass nails!"

"Spangles!" repeated Nelly in surprise; "no one can fasten down a carpet with spangles!"

"It's the look of the thing that I care for," said Matty, who had evidently become a very apt pupil of Folly. "And now I'll tell you where I'm going, Nelly. I have long thought, you know, that a pretty tambourine would look wonderfully well in my parlour; and I think, if I could buy one cheap, that a French picture would give it a fashionable air. I am going on a purchasing expedition, dear Miss Folly being my guide."

"Oh, Matty!" exclaimed Nelly, "you know that you have not yet bought half the things that you require from Mr. Arithmetic the ironmonger!"

"I wish Mr. Arithmetic at Jericho!" cried Matty peevishly; "his goods are so heavyso uninteresting; they make no show; I won't plague myself with such things!"

"Matty, Matty, my beauty!" called the shrill voice of Folly from without.

"I'm coming in a moment," cried Matty, as she hastened to join her companion.

Sadly, but with quiet resolution, Nelly took up her hammer again. Not many minutes had passed before she received a visit from Dick.

"How long are you going to keep on knocking in those dates?" exclaimed the boy; "I put in all mine long ago. You see," he added with a merry laugh, as he held up his hands, "I've nails at my fingers' ends!"

Nelly, who did not quite understand the joke, and was too honest to pretend that she did so, bent down again over her work.

"I can't think how you are so slow!" cried Dick. "I've heard you hammer, hammer, hammering for such a time, that I expected when I came in to find your carpet studded all over with dates, and you have not put in more than six!"

"I am sorry that I am so slow and stupid," said Nelly, with a sigh; "it is not my fault but my misfortune."

Dick felt a little repentant for his unkind and thoughtless words. "I must say, Nelly," he observed, "that slow as you are, your cottage is far better furnished than Matty's, though she is so active and bright. What a lot of trash she has stuffed into her rooms! And such a lovely cottage she has! If the inside only matched the outside, it would be charming indeed!"

"Dear Matty would have furnished her house very nicely," said Nelly, "if Miss Folly had not come in the way."

"Ah, yes! Folly is at the bottom of the mischief!" cried Dick. "How absurdly she has made Matty dress; what numbers of good hours has the silly girl spent in making herself look ridiculous!"

"Oh, don't be hard on Matty!" cried her sister.

"Would you believe it!" said Dick, "Miss Folly has persuaded her to get not only her carpet, but her chairs and tables also, from Mr. Fiction! They are as slight as if made of pasteboard, and won't stand a single week's wear! Now my furniture is good and substantial, and was very reasonable in price besides."

"Where did you get it?" asked Nelly.

"Oh, you know, where Mr. Learning recommended us to go. I buy my furniture from the upholsterer, General Knowledge, whose shop adjoins Mr. Reading's."

"The immense warehouse of facts," said Nelly.

"You may well call it immense," cried Dick; "I believe that it would take one a lifetime to go thoroughly over the place. There are vaults below full of furniture facts; rooms beyond rooms stuffed with facts; mount the stairs, and you'll find story upon story all filled with valuable facts! I assure you, Nelly, that it is a very curious and interesting place to visit, and I never go to General Knowledge without carrying back something well worth the having. I'm just on my way to him now."

"I should like to go with you," said Nelly; "I shall want beds, tables, and chairs; and as I can't carry much at once, I shall need to go very often to the warehouse."

"Come then now, and be quick!" cried Dick, who was, as usual, impatient to start.

"I thinkindeed I am sure," replied Nelly, "that Duty would advise me first to finish the task which I have begun. If other furniture were brought in just now, I might find it harder to nail down my carpet."

"Goodbye, dear drudge!" cried Dick; "I believe that it would be better for us all if we stuck to the counsels of Duty as steadily as you always do! But you see I'm a quick, sharp fellow, and don't like to be tied down by rules; I get what I will, when I will, and where I will; and depend on't, in the end I'll win the crown of Success, for no cottage of Head will be found so wellfurnished as mine!"

And with this somewhat conceited speech on his tongue, off darted our clever young Dick, ran down hill Puzzle at speed, and lightly sprang over brook Bother!

Back to contents

CHAPTER XX.

THE PURSUED BIRD.

“THERE is no doubt but that Dick will be the one to win the crown," was the silent reflection of Nelly; "I work from no hopes of getting that; but it will be quite reward enough for me if my dear mother be pleased with my cottage; and smiles from Duty and Affection would make any labour seem light."

By dint of steady hammering Nelly at last managed to fix in a goodly number of dates. When she was satisfied that enough had been done, she rose from her knees, and relieved herself by a yawn.

"I will go and see after my Plainwork," said she; "the fruit upon it is swelling quite bigI am glad that it will be perfectly ripe when my dear mother comes back. If she be satisfied with it, how little shall I grudge my past troublehow joyful and happy I shall be!"

Nelly uttered these words as she crossed her threshold, and felt the fresh, pleasant air playing upon her flushed cheek and her aching brow.

At that moment her ear caught a whirring sound, as of wings, and looking upwards, she beheld a beautiful bird pursued by a hawk darting down towards her at the utmost speed that terror could lend it. Scarcely had she seen its danger, when the little fluttering fugitive had sought shelter in the bosom of the child.

"Oh, poor little birdpoor little birdthe hawk shall not catch you!" cried Nelly, putting one hand over the trembling creature, and holding out the other to keep the fierce pursuer away.

The hawk, which was of a species called "Tempers," not altogether unknown in Great Britain (my readers may, perhaps, have seen specimens), wheeled round and round in circles, as if unwilling to give up its prey. Nelly was quite afraid that it might attack her, and still pressing the poor frightened bird to her bosom, she hurried back into her cottage.

"You are safe, pretty creaturequite safe. You need no longer tremble and flutter," said the little girl to the bird. It almost seemed as if the fugitive understood her; it spread its pinions, but not to fly away; lightly it hopped on to her hand, and rubbed its soft head against her shoulder.

"I never saw such a beauty of a bird!" cried the delighted Nelly; "and it seems just as tame as it is pretty. What lovely white silvery wings, what soft eyes that gleam like rubies, the changing tints on its neck and breast are lovelier than anything I ever saw before!"

Still perched on her hand, the bird opened his beak, and began to warble a song of gratitude far sweeter than any nightingale's lay. Little Nelly was enraptured at the sound.

"Oh, how glad I am," she exclaimed, "that I did not leave my hammering beforethat I did not go, as I much wished to go, either with Lubin or Dick. This lovely creature would then have been torn to pieces by the cruel hawk, and I should have seen nothing of it, except perhaps a few stained feathers at my door."

"I hear the wellknown warble of my bird Content!" cried a voice from without which Nelly at once recognized; and running to open the door as fast as her lameness would let her, she joyfully admitted her two friends, Affection and Duty.

Content fluttered to the hand of his mistress, Duty.

"Ah, truant!" cried the fair maiden, as she caressed her little favourite, "how could you wander from mehow could you ever fancy yourself safe apart from Duty? I saw the hawk wheeling in the air, and I trembled for my beautiful pet; but he has found here a refuge and protector. Nelly, I thank you for your kindness, and it is with pleasure that I reward it. You have saved the bird, and the bird shall be yours. Go, pretty warbler, go; and, warned by former danger, keep close to your new young mistress."

Nelly uttered an exclamation of delight, as, obedient to the word, silverwinged Content flew again into her bosom, and nestled there like a child.

"Oh, thanks, thanks!" she cried; "such a treasure as this will be a constant delight. I would rather have the bird Content, than even the crown of Success."

"You must never part with it," said Duty earnestly, "whoever may tempt you to do so; my gift must never be sold or exchanged. Content is a wonderful bird; joy and happiness breathe in his note. Though I be not visibly present, such a mysterious tie connects Content with Duty, that when you have followed my rules, and acted as I would have you act, my bird will cheer and reward you with one of his sweetest songs."

"I will never, never part with him of my own free will," said Nelly, as she fondled her bird.

Affection now came forward. The reader may remark that the sisters seemed ever to keep close together, as though they scarcely could live apart. They were indeed tenderly attached, and felt a pleasure in each other's society which made them never willingly sundered. Duty felt that without Affection she would find every occupation a weary task; and Affection, who was a little given to extravagance, would often have got into trouble without the quiet counsels of Duty. Each looked fairer and brighter when seen in the company of her sister.

Affection now placed before Nelly a Book, wrapped in a cover of gold. "To my sister's gift," she said, "I must add one yet more precious. However well the head may be furnished, if the highest knowledge be wanting, all other things become worthless and vain. Treasure this Book, dear child; make it your counsellor and guide; you will not prize it less because Duty requires you to study it, and it may be pleasant to you to remember that you first received it from my hand as the best, the noblest gift which even Affection could offer."

Youthful reader, do you know that Book, and do you dearly prize it? It is that volume which gives knowledge compared to which all the inventions of science, all the learning of man, all the wisdom of this world, is but as dust in the balance.

Back to contents

CHAPTER XXI.

PLANS AND PLOTS.

HOW happy was little Nelly now, with Content as her constant companion. He was with her when she went on expeditions to the town of Education, flying before her, then stopping to rest on some bush by the wayside to cheer her by his musical song. When she returned home laden with furniture, facts from the warehouse of General Knowledge, or some of Arithmetic's more heavy productions, the way seemed shorter, the burden more light when Content was fluttering near. When the four Desleys at last took up their abode in their four little homes, the presence of beautiful Content made Nelly's as bright as a palace.

It is time that I should say something about the gardens which lay behind the cottages of Head, and which were to be cultivated by the children. These were very curiously laid out, according to the plans given by Geography, the celebrated gardener. Each garden represented a map. There were plots of green grass for the sea, dotted with daisies for tiny islands. There was rich dark mould for the land, and flowers or small bushes were planted wherever the capitals of countries should be. Dick, who was very ingenious, contrived to have some characteristic plant for most of those cities.

"See," he exclaimed, "there is a rosebush for London, a thistle for bonny Edinburgh, and a patch of green shamrock for Dublin. I'm getting a lily for Paris, as that is the capital of France; and as Holland is famous for tulips, Amsterdam a tulip shall be."

"And what will you give Belgium?" inquired Matty.

"Brussels sprouts, to be sure."

Dick worked early and late at his garden, and it was by far the finest of the four; even in the season of autumn the difference was very marked. Lubin was so often sauntering off to Amusement's bazaar, and spending his hours at one of her counters, that Geography the gardener grew quite out of patience with him. Lubin quite forgot where to put in the tiny box hedges which marked the boundaries of various countries, so that France spread half over Germany, and swallowed up poor little Belgium altogether. "Italy," as Dick laughingly observed, "was shaped like a gouty shoe, instead of a long slender boot;" and so much grass overran the border, that Matty was certain that all Lubin's land would soon be drowned by the sea. London, Edinburgh, and Paris were dying for want of watering, and nothing seemed to flourish in Lubin's Europe but such things as groundsel and chickweed.

Matty at first succeeded far better with her flowers. She had a taste for gardening, she said, and laid out her map very nicely. Whatever accorded with her inclination, Matty did quickly and well; but she worked from no regard to Duty, and whenever she felt a little tired, she threw down her spade, and went to amuse herself with touching her new tambourine, or blowing bubbles of Fancy with Folly. Yet, upon the whole, Matty's garden was fair and pleasant to behold.

Nelly, who was lame, and had little strength for hard work, found gardening a serious task. It took her long to lay out the plots, long to plant the box hedges; and watering the cities, and keeping the ground clear of weeds seemed an endless business to Nelly. Yet cheerfully and bravely she worked, while, perched on a bush beside her, the beautiful bird Content poured forth enlivening lays. The harder she laboured, the louder sang he; and whenever she glanced up from her task, she saw the gleam of his silver wing reflecting the sunshine from heaven.

"Oh, dear little bird!" cried Nelly, "with what a song will you welcome my mother, who will soon return to us now. How she will stroke your soft feathers, and delight in your cheerful lay! Then, perhaps, thoughtful Duty and sweet Affection will come and remain as my guests, and fill my home with peace and with gladness when chill winter darkens around. Oh, how happily shall we all then gather around our blazing Christmas fire!"

It seems strange that so kind and gentlc a child as Nelly should ever have an enemy; but she was certainly an object of envy and dislike both to Miss Folly and Pride.

"I hate that sober, sensible little minx, who is always thinking of Affection and Duty," said Miss Folly one day to Pride, as they were walking in a thicket together, just as the damp evening mist was beginning to fall.

"I hate her heartily," muttered Pride between his clenched teeth; "for she not only shuts her own door against me, but tries with all the power that she has to weaken my influence with her brothers and sister. She has not succeeded, and she shall not; but I never forget a wrong, and I'd give anything in the world to be able to spite and vex her."

"It drives me wild to hear that bird of hers always singing so gaily!" cried Folly.

"Could we not wring its neck?" exclaimed Pride.

"We dare not so much as touch it without her leave," said Miss Folly, shaking her peacock plume with vexation; "and yet I'd rather make myself a headdress of its feathers than of those of any other bird of the air."

"We'll get hold of it, and kill it without mercy!" cried ugly Pride, grinding his teeth as he spoke; "but we must work by cunning, for we dare not use force, the child is under such powerful protection."

"I'll coax Nelly to part with her bird," said Folly; and rolling her goggle eyes, she added, "you know that I'm a rare hand at coaxing."

"There are few who can withstand you," answered the dark one; his words made Folly simper, she knew not how to blush. "And if," continued Pride, "you succeed, you will make Nelly mortally offend both Duty and Affection; and to break with friends such as they are, will make her miserable indeed."

"She'll only need a good big bribe," said Folly. "I believe that Matty would part with the dearest friend that she has for the sake of a few bright ribbons, or a bunch of fine feathers to wear."

"But Matty is not Nelly," observed Pride.

"Oh, Nelly is only a girl!" cried Folly, tossing her frizzled head, "and there never yet was a girl that could not be wheedled by Folly into doing the silliest thing in the world. If I persuaded Matty that Fashion required her to tattoo her nose all over, to dye her hair green, or blue, or mauve, or to walk on all fours like a cat,don't you suppose that she would do it?"

Pride only shrugged his shoulders in reply.

"Haven't I coaxed Chinese ladies to torture their babies by squeezing their feet into shoes so small, that the halflamed creatures could never, throughout life, walk except in a waddle? Have I not"

"You have done all sorts of wonderful things," said Pride; "no one doubts your power of persuading. Try now your arts upon Nelly, get her to give up her bird, and strangle Content as soon as you get it under your dainty fingers. If you shall be baffled, I will try next; 'twill be strange indeed if a simple child like Nelly be able to withstand us both."

"No fear of that!" exclaimed Folly.

So the two conspirators parted, equally resolved, by any possible means, to effect their object. It was not the first time that Folly and Pride had consulted together how to bring sorrow and shame into a young loving heart; not the first time that they had agreed to use their utmost efforts to destroy a bright and beautiful creature, and silence for ever in death the warbling voice of Content.

Back to contents

CHAPTER XXII.

THE COCKATOO, PARADE.

“GOOD morning to you, sweet Nelly, dear industrious Nelly!" was the greeting of Folly on the following morning, as she stood with a red cockatoo on her wrist, quite filling up Nelly's doorway with her iron hoop and her flounces.

Nelly was busily engaged in screwing on the legs of a table made of facts from Natural History, which she had bought from General Knowledge. A very curious table it was: the facts were as numerous, and fitted together as closely, as the bits of wood in a Tunbridgeware box; and the legs were carved all over with figures of birds and beasts. That table had cost many hours, and had been carried home bit by bit; it was one of the prettiest and handsomest pieces of furniture which appeared in the little cottage.

"Good morning," replied Nelly very coldly, in answer to the salutation; she had no good opinion of Miss Folly, and hoped that she did not intend to linger. Folly had, however, come with an object, and did not appear to notice the coldness of the child, indeed no one is slower than Folly in taking a hint to depart.

"I see that you are as fond of creatures as I am," cried Miss Folly, turning her goggle eyes upon her parrot; "I have a fancy, I may say a passion, for them! I keep a regular 'happy family' at homedogs, cats, mice, parrots, and pigeons, and a little pet alligator, the dearest duck of an alligator, that I've taught to eat out of my hand! You must really come and see them all one day."

"Thank you, but I'm very busy," replied poor Nelly, who wished that her jabbering visitor would leave her in quiet to work.

"But I've no bird like your Content; I really think that I must add it to my collection," said Folly; "it seems to me quite unique!"

Nelly had no notion what unique could mean, but she had a great notion that her Content should never be added to Miss Folly's "happy family."

"Now I've just been thinking," continued the chatterer, "that it would be a nice plana most charming plan, for you and me to make a little exchange. You give me your bird Content, which I'll always cherish and coddle, and feed on sugarplums and strawberry ice, in affectionate remembrance of you"(O Folly! Folly! how little you care for truth!)"and you shall have my magnificent cockatoo, Parade, that I've taught to speak myself; he's the finest creature in the world: you shall hear how clever he is!"

Folly coaxed the bird on her wrist, called him by a dozen pretty names, smiled at him, nodded to him, whistled for him, and at length induced him to speak. The cockatoo bobbed his head up and down, shook his wings, puffed out his red feathers, and then in harsh, sharp tones repeated about a dozen times the sentence, "Pretty Poll! ain't I fine? ain't I fine?"

The bird Content, perched on the mantelpiece, seemed listening in wonder to a voice so unlike his own.

"That is a clever cockatoo," said Nelly, with a smile; "but I would not exchange my Content for any other bird in the world."

"Ah, but Parade is a beautya real beauty!" cried Miss Folly; "Lady Fashion, my most particular friend, would give anything to possess him! I assure you that when I put him in my window, every passerby stops to stare at the creature. Only just hear him again."

And again Parade bobbed his head up and down, swelled himself out, and repeated, "Pretty Poll! ain't I fine? ain't I fine?"

"I protest," cried Folly, speaking faster than ever, "he'll sometimes keep repeating over that sentence from morning till night!"

Nelly was too polite to say it aloud, but she thought that one might get very weary of hearing "Pretty Poll! ain't I fine? ain't I fine?"

"I really do not wish to make any exchange," said the lame girl with mild decision; "Parade has very bright colours, it is true, but I love better the silver wings and soft note of my pretty Content."

Even Folly could not but see that this her first effort had failed; but Folly is not easily discouraged. "If this stupid girl do not care for Parade," thought she, "I'll find something else that she cares for;" and putting the cockatoo down on the table, Folly drew a gay jewelcase from her pocket.

"What do you say to these?" she exclaimed, opening the case, and drawing from it a long string of what looked like pearls, with a sparkling clasp which seemed to be made of diamonds.

"They are very pretty indeed!" said Nelly.

"And so becomingso charmingly becoming! I assure you, my dear, if you would only let me dress up your hair, put it back à l'Imperatrice, and adorn it with these lovely pearls, there's not a creature that would know you again!"

Nelly laughed, and Folly thought that she had now found a vulnerable point; that, like the crow in the fable, the child could be caught by flattery.

"You don't do justice to yourself, my dear; your dress is so common and plain that no one guesses how well you would look if you attended a little to style. If you wore such clothes as Matty now wears, and carried them off with an air, you may depend on't that people would take you for a very grand lady indeed!"

"But why should I wish to be taken for what I am not?" asked Nelly simply.

"My dear, what an absurd question! Does not every one wish to be taken for somebody grander than herself?" cried Folly, jabbering at railroad speed. "The child of the dogs' meat man wears a necklace and hoop; the farmer's daughter cuts out the squire's; the kitchenmaids on Sundays deck out as ladies; each one mimics some one above her, and wants to cut a dash in the world! If any one were content to appear really what she is, I should cut her society at once; I should let the whole world know that she had nothing to do with Folly!"

Sharing the excitement of his mistress, "Ain't I fine? ain't I fine?" cried Parade.

"Now, my dear, I'll tell you what I'll do," continued Folly, lowering her voice to a confidential tone; "you shall give me your bird Content, and, as I told you before, I shall feed him and foster him with the same care as I do my own pet alligator. In return I will not only present you with this charming string of pearls, but will show you how to wear them in a manner the most bewitching."

"I do not think that pearls would suit a plain little girl like me!"

"Plain! if ever I heard such a thing. You've a countenance quite out of the common! You've the prettiest nosethe sweetest little nose; and as for your smile!" Folly threw up her hands, and cast up her eyes, to denote admiration too great to be expressed by mere words.

Poor little Nelly was rather taken aback by praises to which she had not been accustomed. She certainly placed little confidence in anything said by her visitor; yet flattery has some sweetness in it, even from the lips of Folly. Let no little girl who reads my story despise poor Nelly for smiling and blushing, unless she be quite certain that she never herself has done the same on a similar occasion. But Nelly, though amused, was not caught even by the bait of the pearls and the praises. She remembered many a word of sensible advice given by her faithful friend Duty, and drawing a little back from Folly, who in her eager confidential manner had pressed up quite close to the child, she said in a modest tone, "Whatever our looks may be, a simple and sober dress, such as suits our age and station, is what Duty always recommends."

"Dutythe old horror!" exclaimed Folly, who could not endure the very name; "I don't wonder that you're formal and quiet, if you tie yourself down to her laws. No, no, my pretty Nell, you must break away at once from such a dull, tiresome guide; don't talk to me of Duty again! I'll take you under my charge; I'll show you all my delights; I'll even" here Folly again lowered her voice to a confidential tone, and leant forward her frizzled head as she whispered, "I'll even manage to introduce you to my most particular friend, Lady Fashion!"

"Nothing on earth would make me give up Duty!" exclaimed Nelly warmly, for she could bear no word spoken against her friend. "I will never forget her, nor part with her gift; and I don't want, indeed I don't, to be introduced to Lady Fashion!"

Miss Folly started back in indignation and horror. "Not want to be introduced to Lady Fashion! the girl must be out of her senses! Not one moment longer shall Folly condescend to stay near one who has the effrontery to own that she does not want to be introduced to Lady Fashion!" and, snatching up her cockatoo, Parade, Miss Folly rushed out of the cottage as fast as her mass of frippery would let her.

Nelly looked after her with a wondering smile, and Content, perched on the shoulder of his young mistress, burst forth into the merriest of songs.

Miss Folly did not stop in her running till she arrived, out of breath, at the spot where Pride was awaiting her return.

"What success?" asked the dark one, though he saw at a glance that Folly had been baffled and defeated.

"I'll never go near her again!" gasped forth Folly; "I'll never put my foot across her threshold! She has disappointed me, rejected me, insulted me; she does not care for my cockatoo, Parade, nor wish to be introduced to my most particular friend, Lady Fashion!" and Folly almost cried with spite and vexation.

"She will not escape me so easily," said Pride; "my arts are deeper than yours. I have resolved that her bird shall die, and die it shall, before tomorrow, let her guard it as well as she may."

"She always keeps Content beside her," observed Folly, "and you know that neither of us are able to take it away by force."

"Not by force," said Pride gloomily, "but by fraud. I know that I cannot with my own hands wring the neck of Content; but I'll do more, I'll make Nelly kill him herself!"

"How can you do that?" exclaimed wondering Folly.

Pride glanced round to see that no one else was listening before he replied, in a voice sunk to a horrible whisper, "I've a poisoned cage, called Ambition, very fair and fine to the eye. Let Content be but once placed in that, and he will swell, and swell, till he burst, like one of your own bubbles, Miss Folly."

Folly looked charmed at the clever idea. "But how to get the bird into the cage?" said she.

"Leave that to me," answered Pride; "I know how to manage these matters. There is many a one who would scorn to listen to the offers of Folly, who cannot turn a deaf ear to Pride. You have power over a weak mind like Matty's, and can turn and mould her at your will; but it needs a more subtle spirit, a more artful lure, to overcome a girl who has been brought up under the guidance of Duty."

Back to contents

CHAPTER XXIII.

THE CAGE OF AMBITION.

"WELL furnished, yet simply furnishedall good, plain, solidthat is what I like and approve!"

Nelly looked up on hearing these words, and her glance became one of surprise when she saw by whom they had been uttered. Pride was standing with folded arms not at the door but at the window; his dark, haughty expression was gone, and he looked mildly down at the child.

"Do not fear me, Nelly," he said, "I shall make no attempt to enter. I know that you have been set against me by those who have little acquaintance with me. I blame them not, they act for the best; and I honour you for following the counsels of such friends as Duty and Affection."

"Really," thought Nelly as she listened, "Pride is not so bad as I took him to be."

"Perhaps," continued the cunning deceiver, "were my character better known, even virtuous Duty herself would find me no foe, but a friend. Mr. Learning I often have served, though he will not acknowledge my services. I have spurred on his cleverest pupil to efforts which, without me, he would never have made."

"But have you not brought Dick into some trouble?" suggested Nelly, glancing timidly up at Pride.

"Such troubles as generous natures encounter, the dangers that await the daringdangers much to be preferred to the inglorious safety of the sluggard. To yourself, Nelly, I appeal, for you are a girl of rare sense; your brave perseverance in labour, your wise use of the bridge of Patience, your attention to the call of Duty, show that you possess a judgment far beyond what might be expected at your age."

"Pride is not half so ugly as I used to fancy that he was," thought Nelly.

"To you I appeal," continued Pride. "Had I possessed the same influence over Lubin as that which I have exercised over his brother, would not the result have been for good? Would not Lubin's cottage have been better furnished, his hours more nobly employed; would he not have scorned to throw away so much money on sweetmeats; would not honest Pride have kept him from the meanness of giving up everything for Amusement?"

"Yes, I believe so," answered Nelly, and she was only speaking the truth; she might have added, however, that no efforts are really noble, no acts really worthy of praise, that are owing, not to a regard for Duty, but to the influence of selfish Pride.

"I could not forbear calling here," continued the deceiver, who felt that his artful words were beginning to make an impression, "to congratulate you, as I do with all my heart, upon your late conduct, so noble and wise."

"Whenwhere?" asked the wondering Nelly.

"I speak of your triumph over Miss Follyover that weak, silly, frivolous creature who has, unhappily, so much power over the minds of ignorant girls. Wise were you, Nelly, most wise, not to exchange your beautiful Content for false pearls or prating Parade. You have a soul above froth and frippery, you despise both flattery and Folly, no one will catch you blowing bubbles of Fancy to furnish a most empty dwelling!"

Nelly began to understand how it was that Dick had found Pride such a pleasant companion.

"Yes," continued the deceiver, leaning through the open window, on the sill of which he rested his arms, "you scorn that poor wretched Parade, that screams 'Ain't I fine?' to each passerby, as if seeking to attract vulgar notice. Independent of others, you can stand by yourself; you have won Content, you prize it, you deserve it; but has it never struck your mind, Nelly, how difficult it may prove for you to keep it?"

"No," replied Nelly, caressing her bird; "I shall never give my favourite away."

"But your favourite may take wing and depart. Do you expect Content to remain in this small cottage, with all the free air to soar in?"

Nelly looked uneasy and anxious, and pressed her bird closer to her heart.

"It is the nature of birds to mount aloft. Trust me, Nelly, Content will not linger long here while he has unrestrained use of his wings."

"I could not bear to lose him!" cried Nelly.

"To save you that pain," said Pride, watching closely her face as he spoke, "see what I have brought for you here!" and he raised and placed on the sill of the window the gilded cage of Ambition.

"Oh, what a splendid, magnificent cage!" cried poor simple Nelly, suspecting no evil; "and did you really intend it for me?"

"See how ready I am to forgive and forget," said Pride, with a wicked, mocking smile, as he saw the guileless child lay her hand on the poisoned gift; "you have spoken against me, tried to drive me awaynay, at this very moment, I believe, you would not suffer me to enter your doorand yet I bring you this cage that you may never lose your Content; that you may see it grow greater and greater, and never fly from your home!"

"You are very good," began Nelly, and stopped short; she was startled at the sound of her own words.

"Yes, I am very good, am I?" laughed Pride, as he turned away from the window, and then began to stalk down the hill, muttering to himself as he walked, "Ay, she will think me very good, doubtless, when she seesas she will see before morningher beautiful, her cherished Content gasping and swelling in the agonies of death!" and as in thought he enjoyed his barbarous triumph, how hideous grew the dark features of Pride.

But the wicked one was blowing the trumpet of victory before the battle had been won! Nelly, indeed, looked with admiration and pleasure upon the glittering cage, and was about to place her favourite within it, when a thought arrested her hand. "My mother has warned us very often to have nothing to do with Pride; Duty has told me again and again that nowhere upon earth could I find a more dangerous companion than he. Ought I to accept this gift? is it suitable, is it right, to take a present from one whom I dare not invite to enter my cottage? Oh, surely I have done wrong in listening with such pleasure to his flattering words! What should I do now; what would Duty counsel me to do? I will return to him his beautiful cage, and keep nothing, however charming, that ever belonged to Pride!"

Catching up the tempting gift, Nelly hastened out of her cottage and saw Pride descending the hill.

"Pride! Pride!" she called out as loudly as she could. The dark one pretended not to hear, and only quickened his steps.

"Oh, how shall I ever overtake him," thought lame Nelly; and again she called, but in vain, while she followed as fast as she could.

"Had I not better keep and use the cage, since it is so hard to return it?" thought Nelly. Inclination bade her go back, and imprison Content within the glittering bars; but the recollection of Duty was strong, and exerting her utmost efforts, the child succeeded in overtaking Pride when he had almost reached brook Bother.

"Oh, take this back," gasped the panting Nelly; "it is fine and tempting, I own, but Duty would not allow me to keep it."

"You don't mean to insult me by returning my gift?" exclaimed Pride, in a tone of fierce disappointment.

"I must do what is right," said Nelly, though frightened by his threatening scowl; "take back your cage of Ambition, I dare give it no place in my home!"

"Thenthere, let it go!" thundered Pride; and snatching up the poisoned cage, he sent it whirling round and round through the air till it fell splashing into brook Bother! "I only wish that I could send you after it!" he exclaimed, and gnashing his teeth with disappointment and fury, Pride rushed away from the spot.

Little Nelly returned up the hill at a much slower pace than that at which she had descended it. Ere she had gone halfway a bright silver wing gleamed through the air, and Content alighted on her shoulder. Perched there, the sweet bird poured forth so loud and joyous a lay that one might fancy that he knew the danger from which he had so narrowly escaped, and was aware of the fact which so many, by bitter experience, have learned, that Content must be poisoned and perish if placed in the gilded cage of Ambition.

Back to contents

CHAPTER XXIV.

A VISIT TO MR. CHEMISTRY.

WITH her bird still warbling on her shoulder, Nelly bent her steps to the cottage of her sister. Matty had cared little for her society of late, but Duty and Affection had both taught Nelly to keep up all family ties. She was going to tell Matty of her little adventure, but Nelly found her too full of her own troubles to care about anything else.

"Such a provoking thing has happened!" exclaimed Matty, who was seated on a very flimsy chair, which she had purchased from Mr. Fiction. It gave such a loud crack as she leant back upon it, that Nelly expected to see it come to pieces beneath the weight of her sister.

"O Matty, I wish that you would buy better furniture from General Knowledge," cried Nelly; "I do believe that in a few weeks those wretched chairs will be fit for nothing but firewood!"

"I did buy a pair of screens from General Knowledge," cried Matty; "I brought them home several weeks ago, as you perhaps may remember."

"Yes, I rccollect," replied Nelly; "they were handsome and valuable screens. One was made of Botany facts, all carved over with leaves and flowers; the other of Biography facts, covered with likenesses of great men. They were really a beautiful pair, but I don't see them now," added Nelly, with an inquiring glance round the room.

"They're lost to me and my heirs for ever!" cried Matty, again tossing herself backwards on her chair, which again gave an ominous creaking.

"How could they be lost?" exclaimed Nelly.

"Stolenstolen by the robber Forgetfulness," answered Matty; "a regular burglar he is! I neglected to lock my door at nightI never dreamed of any dangerand in came the robber and carried away my pair of beautiful screens."

"How very vexatious," exclaimed Nelly.

"Yes, indeed; where's the use of spending hours upon hours in furnishing, and labouring to carry heavy things over brook Bother and up the steep hill of Puzzle, if Forgetfulness sneak in at last and carry the best goods away."

"What use, indeed," echoed Nelly; "the sad warnings of the misfortunes which have happened to you and poor Lubin from Forgetfulness stealing your facts, and Procrastination robbing him of his hours, must make each of us more careful in guarding our treasures from such thieves."

"If Forgetfulness had only taken one of those worthless chairs instead," sighed Matty; "to think of losing the best facts, and keeping the useless fictions."

"How nowwhat's the matter?" cried the cheerful voice of Dick, as he entered Matty's cottage with a brisk lively step; "you look as doleful as Miss Folly did just now when I met her with her red cockatoo on her wrist, appearing so disconsolate and sad that I thought her most particular friend, Lady Fashion, must have died of late hours or tightlacing!"

"Miss Folly disconsolate and sad!" exclaimed Matty; "ah, perhaps she had heard that my poor little cottage had been robbed."

"That was not the cause of her melancholy," said Dick; "I daresay, were the truth to be known, that Miss Folly herself had something to do with the business; for many a day has she been seen in company with Forgetfulness the burglar."

"I'm certain that Folly is perfectly innocent," cried Matty.

"Oh, I don't mean to accuse the fair lady; I only mention what I have heard; you and she may settle the affair between you. But as regards her present vexation, that, Nelly, all lies at your door. It seems that you despised her cockatoo Parade, and would not part with Content in exchange for it. But I've set all matters right; I've taken a fancy to the creature, I've promised to buy it from Folly, and instead of prating for ever, 'Ain't I fine?' I'll teach it to cry, 'Ain't I clever?'"

"And then you'll give it to me!" exclaimed Matty. "There's nothing that I adore like Parade; often and often I've wished to have it. I'm quite astonished that Nelly should prefer that dull, spiritless creature, Content."

"I've done more yet to put Folly into good humour," said Dick, who, though he heartily despised his sister's companion, yet liked to amuse himself sometimes with her airs; "I've invited her to come this evening and see my grand display of fireworks."

"Fireworks! oh, that will be charming!" exclaimed Matty, clapping her hands.

"And I've desired her to bring Pride with her; nothing goes off well without him."

Nelly, who had a disagreeable recollection of her late interview with Pride, looked very grave on hearing of the invitation given to him by her brother.

"Where did you get the fireworks?" asked Matty, who, in her pleasure at the idea of seeing something new, had quite forgotten her loss.

"Where but from Mr. Chemistry? I knew that it was all nonsense in old Learning to say that his goods were not yet for me. Pride and I were laughing half the evening at the sage's oldfashioned notions. I suppose that he thinks that no one can see the world till forced to look at it through spectacles, like himself. 'You need an introduction, indeed!' cried Pride; 'just step up boldly like a man. Mr. Chemistry, with his gases, his retorts, his acids, and his alkalies, will be glad enough to see the colour of your money without making uncivil observations.' Said I, 'Mr. Pride, your advice is good, and I'll act upon it directly.' So off starts I, brave as a lion; plank Patience still lay across brook Bother, but I kicked it right into the stream."

"Oh, why did you do so?" exclaimed Nelly.

"Patience may do well enough for you," replied Dick, "but you see a chap like me doesn't want it. Well, to go on with my story. I found Mr. Chemistry hard at work beside an electric machine, and I stopped some moments to watch the crackling sparks drawn from the whirling glass wheel. At last the old fellow looked up, and saw me with my purse in my hand. 'You're a young student,' says he. 'An old head on young shoulders,' says I, looking as solemn and wise as Mr. Learning himself could do. 'You'll need to undergo a short examination,' says he, 'upon the first principles of my science.' Those words rather took me aback, for I had not counted upon that. 'What's a simple body?' says he, turning over to the first page of a book that was near him. 'A simple body,' says I; 'why, that is my sister Matty, for she's hand and glove with Miss Folly.'"

"O Dick, how could you speak so?" cried Matty.

"I set the old fellow laughing, and then, of course, I got everything my own way. I told him that I did not want science but fireworks, and that I knew that he had them in lots. I wished something that would go hissing, and fizzing, and whizzing, and astonish and dazzle beholders. To make a long story short, I carried off all that I wanted; and I invite you both this evening to see my grand firework display."

"It will be delightfulquite charming," cried Matty; "and my darling Miss Folly to be there!"

"Miss Folly and Pride too," said Dick; "but what makes our Nelly so solemn and grave?" he added, clapping the lame girl on the shoulder.

"O Dick, I should like muchvery muchto see your fireworks, but I cannotindeed, I cannotgo to meet Folly and Pride."

"What nonsense!" exclaimed Dick, impatiently; "if they're good enough company for us, they're surely good enough company for you."

"Both my dear mother and Duty have warned me against such companions; I may not go where they go."

"Stay at home thenno one wants you!" exclaimed Dick, who, puffed up as he was by selfconfidence, could not endure the slightest opposition. "Set yourself up for a model childlame, plain, and stupid as you are."

Poor Nelly's heart swelled as if it would burst at such undeserved rudeness from her brother. She returned, however, no angry word, but silently and quietly quitted the place. Her eyes were so much dimmed by tears, that she could scarcely see her way back to her own little cottage.

"It was a shame in me to speak so to Nelly," exclaimed Dick, who repented of his unkind speech almost as soon as he had uttered it.

"You had better tell her so," said Matty, who, though frivolous and careless, was not an illnatured girl.

Dick turned to follow Nelly, and would doubtless have made all things smooth with his sister, had he not met dark Pride at the door.

Ah, dear reader, have you never been stopped by Pride when going to beg forgiveness of one to whom you knew that you had done a wrong, and especially when that injured party was younger and less clever than yourself?

Dick would not demean himself, as he called it, in the presence of watchful Pride, by telling his little sister that he was sorry for having hurt her feelings. Pride came to talk about the fireworks, and, in eager conversation with him, thoughtless Dick soon forgot the wound which his overbearing temper had inflicted upon a gentle and loving heart.

Back to contents

CHAPTER XXV.

A LESSON.

EVENING was coming on. Poor Nelly sat sad and alone in the parlour of her little cottage. She had seen little of Dick since the morning; and when they had accidentally met, he had not uttered one word of regret for his unkindness. Indeed, his manner had been so careless, that it appeared that what had passed so lately between them had quite gone out of his mind. Nelly tried to forgive and forget, but her spirit was sad and low. Even Content seemed to droop his wing, and would scarcely give even a chirp.

Nelly felt alsoas what girl of her age would not feel!being shutout from the merry little party that were going to enjoy the fireworks. The display, on account of the direction of the wind, was to be close in front of Matty's cottage, instead of that of Dick; and as this dwelling, as we know, adjoined Nelly's, the lame girl from her little window could have but an imperfect view, and would lose all the general effect.

"Perhaps," thought poor Nelly, "I have been needlessly strict after all; I have been a little too particular in doing what I thought that duty might require. I have lost a great deal of pleasure, and I have offended my own dear brother. Everything has seemed gloomy since the morningeven my bird will not sing. Ah, how glad I am that my mother will soon return. I shall never doubt what I ought to do when I have her dear voice to guide me; and I am sure that when she is here, Content will warble from morning till night."

"What, Nelly, here all alone?" said Lubin, putting his round, goodhumoured face in at the door.

Nelly only looked up and smiled, for at that moment she could not speak; and her smile was so sad, that Lubin came in and seated himself at her side.

"Why, you have been crying, Nelly!" he said. "What is the matter with you, dear? Has Forgetfulness robbed you of your choicest facts, or Procrastinationthe sly rogue!stolen your hours, or have you dropped some nice little purchase of yours into the muddy waters of Bother?"

Nelly shook her head in reply to each question. "I have vexed Dick," she answered at last, "by refusing to join his party at the firework display, because he has invited Pride and Miss Folly."

"I daresay that you did quite right," observed Lubin; "though it's rather hard upon you to have to give up the fireworks and fun. You'll hardly see anything from your window. Come to my cottage opposite; there you will have a good view of it all."

"I would rather remain quietly here, dear Lubin; with many thanks to you for the offer. I have no heart for amusement this evening, and would not wish Dick to see me watching, as if by stealth, the fireworks which I would not go openly to view." As Nelly spoke, she could not prevent two large tears, which had been gathering beneath her lashes, from overflowing her eyes.

Lubin, lazy sluggard as he was, yet was a kindhearted boy, and would do a good turn for any one, provided it gave him small trouble. "I'll stay with you, Nelly," he said, kissing the tear from her cheek; "it will be better for me, you know, to keep clear of Folly and Pride." Nelly squeezed his hand to express her thanks. "There is Miss Folly approaching already," continued Lubin. "One might know her coming were she a mile off, by the sound of her jabbering voice."

Lubin rose and went to the window to look out. "Yes; there is Miss Follypeacock plume, balloon dress, and all; and she has a red cockatoo on her wrist. Blackbrowed Pride is behind her. Matty and Dick are running to meet them."

Nelly did not go to the window; but she heard the voices without, which sounded distinctly through the still evening air.

"I wonder if it will ever get dark enough for the lovely, delightful fireworks. I've been wishing all the afternoon that I could push on the sun doublequick to the west. It's always dark when one wants it to be light, and light when one wants it to be dark." My readers will scarcely need to be told that these words were spoken by Folly.

"I'm glad that you've brought your cockatoo," said Dick; "you know that I'm going to buy him."

"He's worth his weight in goldhe is; pretty creature!just listen to him now!" And Nelly could hear the harsh, grating voice of Parade: "Pretty Poll! ain't I fine? ain't I fine?"

"I'm going to teach him something else," observed Dick. "Just let me have him here for a few minutes. The fireworks are ready prepared, but we must wait till the twilight grows darker. In the meantime, I will amuse myself by giving Master Cockatoo a lesson in talking."

"You'll soon make him say what you like," observed Pride.

"Isn't it a beautiful bird?" cried Matty.

"They are gathering round the cockatoo, Nelly," said Lubin, who was still at the window. "Only Miss Folly, with her painted face and goggle eyes, is peeping at the preparations for the fireworks."

The last faint tinge of red had faded from the sky. Deeper and deeper grew the gathering shades. Lubin could scarcely distinguish the features of the group that were amusing themselves with Parade.

"Now, my good cockatoo," began Dick, standing in front of his redfeathered pupil, "you know 'variety is charming,' says the proverb. We may like to hear you say the same thing over nine hundred and ninetynine times; but when a question is asked for the thousandth time, we begin to wish for a little variation. Suppose now, just for a change, you say, 'Ain't I clever? ain't I clever?'"

"Ain't I fine?ain't I fine?" screamed Parade.

"Fine? Yes, we know that you are; dark as it is growing, we see that you are; it's a fact which no one will dispute. But just try now"

Dick had not time to conclude his sentence. Bang!crash!there was a loud deafening noise, as if a cannon had been suddenly fired at their ears. Nelly started in terror to her feet, and rushed to the window to see what had happenedfrightened by the shrieks and cries which succeeded the terrible explosion, that had smashed every pane of glass in the cottages! The whole air was full of thick smoke, through which Nelly beheld Miss Folly, with her flounces all on fire, rushing wildly into the dwelling of Dick, which was just opposite to that of Matty.

"O Lubin! something terrible has happened. Plunge the tablecover into that pailful of waterlet us fly to saveoh, help! help!"

Back again through Dick's doorway rushed screaming Miss Folly, after having set fire to his curtains within. Happily she was met by Lubin and Nelly, who threw over her flaming, flaring dress the damp folds of the dripping tablecover. She struggled fiercely to get away from them, as though she thought that they meant to smother her; and it was with the utmost difficulty that the two succeeded in throwing Folly on the ground, and putting out the flames entirely, by rolling her round and round in the mire.

Matty's screams of alarm mingled with those of Miss Folly; and not without cause, for the explosion had set fire to the thatch of her cottage; and through the windows of Dick's came a terrible fiery glowhis furniture was all in a blaze. The whole scene around was as light as day in the fierce red glare of the burning.

Happily assistance was nearvery near. Duty and Affection had been ascending the hill to pay an evening visit to Nelly, when they had been startled by the noise of the explosion, the shrieks, and then the sight of the blazing thatch. Without a moment's delay they had shouted for assistance to a party of men who were going homewards at the close of a day's work. A cart full of empty barrels happened to be passing at the same time, and its contents were instantly seized upon for use. The labourers, incited and directed by the sisters, rushed down at once to the brook, thankful that water was so nigh. Happily there was no wind to fan the fierce conflagration, a heavy mist was beginning to rise, and strong and willing hands were at work to put out the fire. Duty and Affection were everywhereencouraging the men, directing their efforts, nay, labouring themselves with an energy and courage which filled all beholders with surprise. Never could Nelly forget that night. The rushing to and frothe crackling of the flamesthe hissing of the water thrown upon themthe volumes of smoke that arose, the cries, the screams, the hallooingthen the shout of triumph when at length the fire was completely subdued.

Nelly's chief alarm was on account of her brother and sister. While the tumult yet raged around, she rushed, guided by Matty's screams, to a spot where she found the poor girl trembling in an agony of terror.

"Oh, Matty, are you injured?" exclaimed Nelly.

"I don't knowI can't tell," sobbed Matty, who was much more frightened than hurt, though her hair, and even her eyebrows, had been singed by the explosion of the fireworks.

"And Dickpoor Dickis he safe?" cried Nelly, glancing anxiously around.

"There he islying on the ground!" exclaimed Lubin, who had just discovered his brother stretched senseless upon the earth, having been struck on the head by a large piece of wood at the time of the explosion.

"Oh, I hope and trust that he is not killed!" exclaimed Nelly, running to him, in bitter distress.

"Not killed, only stunnedsee, he is opening his eyes," said Lubin, who was now on his knees, supporting his brother in his arms. "If Matty would only assist us, we could carry him into your cottage, Nelly, out of this noise and confusion."

Tenderly the three young Desleys raised their poor wounded brother, and carried him into the cottage. Affection soon followed, to attend to his hurts and bind up his bleeding browfor Affection is a nurse of great skill.

The fire was outthe danger over; Duty rewarded the labourers, and the cottages were left to the children and their two faithful friends in need. Duty and Affection remained through all the dark hours of that trying night, soothing Matty, encouraging Lubin, cheering the heart of poor Nelly. Even when obliged to leave for awhile, the sisters paid repeated visits to the cottage, bearing with them everything needful. Nelly now found, indeed, what it was to have such friends as Duty and Affection.

Dick's injury had brought on brainfever. For three days and nights Nelly scarcely quitted her brother. All his unkindness was quite forgotten, and she would not have left her place at his side for ought that the world could give. Dick had been severely, though not dangerously, hurt. It would be some time, the doctor said, before he would be fit for any exertion. Books must be kept from his sight; he must not, for weeks to come, be allowed to visit the town of Education. But his life had been happily spared; gradually his strength would return. Nelly did not like to tell the poor invalid that all the furniture of his cottage, which he had regarded with so much satisfaction, had been destroyed by the fire; nor that poor Matty's thatch had been burned, and her pretty white wall all blackened and scorched by the flame.

Dear reader! should you ever be tempted to harbour Pride, on account of a wellfurnished head or a beautiful faceoh, remember how soon the fairest features may be made unsightly, the most talented mind rendered feeble and weak, by a sudden accident or fever. The labours of years may be swept awaythe highest powers rendered useless; and one whom all admire today, may be but an object of pity tomorrow.

Back to contents

CHAPTER XXVI.

HEARING THE TRUTH.

IT was not until Dick was able to sit up, propped by cushions, in an armchair, that Nelly could be persuaded by Lubin to make a little expedition with him to buy some things needful for their mother, whose arrival in two days was expected. Lubin liked to do nothing by himself; he would not have taken the trouble to cross brook Bother unless a sister had been at his side; and poor Matty had positively refused to go, as she disliked showing herself to strangers while her hair and eyebrows were so sadly disfigured by the fire.

"Please, Matty," said Nelly, before she set out, "see that poor Dick wants nothing during my absence. Perhaps you would sit beside him. But, pray, say nothing to him that can possibly vex or excite him; you know that he is still very weak, and the fever might possibly return."

Matty agreed to play the nurse for an hour, and with a slow and lingering step she accordingly went to the cottage in which her brother was staying.

It was sad to see the young, bright, active boy placed like an aged man in an armchair, his cheek, so lately glowing with health, almost as pale as the pillow upon which it was resting. Dick's eye was, however, still bright, and he had his old playfulness of manner, though his tone was more feeble than usual, as he exclaimed, on the entrance of his sister, "Why, Matty, you and I look for all the world as if we had been in the wars! I with this bandage across my brow, you with your hair cropped close, and your eyebrows all singed off; you can't think how funny you look!"

Poor Matty hid her face with her hands, and was ready to burst into tears.

"Oh, don't take it to heart!" cried Dick; "hair will soon grow again, you know. I wonder that your friend Miss Folly has not helped you to an elegant wig."

"She is no friend of mine!" exclaimed Matty, with vehemence. "Do you not know that it was Folly who caused the explosion? She thought, like an idiot as she is, that it would be fun to put a match to the fireworks when all our backs were turned, and make us start with surprise. It was her meddling that caused all this mischief and misery;" and again poor disfigured Matty hid her face in her hands.

"Then I hope that you'll cut her from this day forth," observed Dick.

"She has cut us," replied Matty, quickly. "Have you not heard how her flounces were all in a blaze, and how she rushed about as if mad, into a cottage and out again, till Nelly and Lubin knocked her down just in time to save her from being quite burned?"

"I have heard nothing," said Dick, raising himself on his chair, with an expression of curiosity and interest; "you know that Nelly has been my nurse, and she would hardly speak a word for fear lest she should put me into a fever."

Matty was eager to impart all her knowledge, quite regardless of Nelly's parting warning, and began to talk so fast that Dick could not help being reminded of poor Miss Folly.

"Well, you shall hear everything now. Folly was knocked down, or pulled down, as I said, and then rolled about in the mud, till you could hardly have distinguished her head from her feet, or her peacock's plume from a cow's tail. And very thankful and very much delighted she ought to have been, for, if she had been quite choked with mire, it would have been better than burning alive!"

"A painful choice," observed Dick.

"But she was not choked to death," continued Matty; "she was not hurt the least bit; and yetwould you believe it?Miss Folly is in a most furious rage against those who saved her. She declares that she ought to have a lawsuit against Nelly and Lubin to recover the value of her clothes, and another to get them punished for knocking her into the mud; and she has promised a thousand times never to come near one of our family again."

"I hope," said Dick, with a smile, "that for once Miss Folly may keep her promise. But what has become of her red cockatoo?"

"Ah, there's another great grievance!" cried Matty. "The bird must have been frightened by the explosion; and no wonder, for a terrible sight it was, and a horrible noise it made. Parade has flown off, no one knows whither; and though papers and placards about him have been put up in every direction, offering no end of rewards to whoever will bring him back, the bird is not to be found. Folly says, that poor innocent I must have hidden him somewhere from view; but I am sure that I have not even a guess whither the gaudy creature has fled!"

"Had you hidden him," observed Dick Desley, "Parade would soon have betrayed you by screaming out 'Ain't I fine?' And what has become of Pride?"

"Some say," replied Matty, "that he got a great blow on the nose at the time of the explosion; others say that he was not at all injured by it. He certainly did not help Duty to put out the fire. All that I know of Pride is, that he came to our villas this morning, and walked straight up to yours, I suppose from its being the one which he had been most accustomed to visit. I saw him from my window, standing awhile with folded arms, gloomily surveying the place; he then shrugged his shoulders, said, 'What a wreck!' and instantly stalked away."

"What did he mean by exclaiming 'What a wreck?'" asked Dick, with a look of surprise.

"He meant your poor cottage, of course," replied Matty; "all its furniture burned and destroyed."

"Howwhat?" exclaimed Dick in a startled tone; "the fire was not in my cottage at all; the explosion took place by yours."

"I know that too well," sighed poor Matty; "but Folly rushed straight into your home, blazing away like a rocket, then rushed out again, but not before she had set your curtains on fire."

"Do you mean that all my furniture is burned!" exclaimed Dick, striking his fist with violence upon a table that was near him.

"Burned to a cinder," replied Matty; "there's scarcely anything left but the grates."

"The carpetthe splendid carpet destroyed too?" cried poor Dick, starting upright on his feet.

"Great holes burned in every part, and all the dates as black as charcoal!"

Dick sank back on his seat with a groan.

"The beautifully papered walls," continued Matty, "not fit to be looked at now; the fine furniturefacts mere charred wood, or little heaps of gray ashes!"

"And mother coming back the day after tomorrow!" exclaimed Dick, with a burst of anguish. "And doubtless Mr. Learning will come with her, bringing the crown of Success for which I have laboured so hard! I must go at once to the town," he cried wildly; "I must work, work hard till they appear!" And springing from his chair he made an effort to walk; but the limbs, once so active and strong, would no longer support his weight, and, overcome with vexation, Dick tottered back into his seat.

"I can't do it," he cried; "I can't go! Oh, misery and disappointment! Leave me, Matty, leave me; remain no longer with a wretched boy who has lost everything that he valued!"

Matty was frightened at the vehement storm of passion which her indiscretion had raised; and being quite unable to speak a word of comfort to her brother, she crept out of the cottage, feeling more unhappy than when she had entered it.

Back to contents

CHAPTER XXVII.

A BRAVE EFFORT.

“OH! why should this bewhy should this be?" groaned Dick, as soon as he found himself alone; "why should I, the genius of the family, suddenly find myself reduced to the state of the veriest dunce? Why should one wretched accident take from me more than Matty lost by Forgetfulness, or Lubin by Procrastination? Why should I have a cottage so ruined and emptyI who had made its furniture my gloryI who had worked so hard and so well?"

It is a wise thing for those in trouble to try and search for the reason of their trials. No sorrow is sent without a cause. Dick sat long with his brow leaning on his hand, thinking, and thinking, and seeking as well as his poor, languid mind would let him, to trace out his past career.

Why had he worked so hardwhy had he worked so well? Was it indeed for the sake of his mother, or from regard to Mr. Learning, or because he had been taught by Duty in all things to do his best? Dick looked round upon Nelly's little room; every article there reminded him of patient perseverance, of steady application, not because labour had been easy and pleasant, but because she had felt it to be right. Dick, who was a very intelligent boy, could not but see, now that reflection was forced upon him, that he had spent his hours and furnished his cottage only to please and enrich himself, to triumph over his brother and sisters, to gain the silver crown of Success, and to gratify evil Pride! Yes, Pride had urged him to every effort: Pride had made him resolve that no cottage should be as splendidly furnished as his own; Pride had dogged his steps, directed his labours, had introduced him to mischievous Folly, and, worst of all, had made him look down on his best friends and nearest relations, and insult his gentle little sister! Ah! this was the bitterest reflection of all!

"How Pride used to make me laugh at the laziness of Lubin, the vanity of Matty, the lameness of my dear little Nelly, though that was no fault of her own. I remember now but too well that it was through him that I insulted the sister whose talents might be less than mine, but whose virtues should have been my example. It was Pride who made me ashamed to ask forgiveness, or express regret for words as unjust as they were unkind. Yes, this sore trial must have been sent to warn me that he who takes Pride as his bosom companion will sooner or later repent of having done so. What Pride can offer is but a sorry exchange for the peace, the harmony, the love which it seems his delight to destroy! Was it Pride who nursed me through my illness? Was it Pride who so gently bore with my wayward humours; who prepared the cooling draught for my fevered lips, and never seemed weary of watching beside me all through the long dreary night? O

Nelly, not one word of reproach did I ever hear from your tongue; but my heart reproaches me the more for having mocked at your tender counsels, given way to impatient temper, and thrown away your love as a worthless thing at the bidding of haughty Pride!"

"Did I not hear my own name?" said a voice at the door, and the beams of the setting sun threw a dark shadow across the threshold. The next moment Pride would have entered, but Dick waved him back with a gesture of command.

"Whatdo you not know your old friend?" cried Pride.

"I know my old tempter," said the boy, with emotion. "Pride, I have lately suffered much, but I have not suffered in vain; I have lost much, but I have gained something alsoa knowledge of myself, and of you! Here let us part, and for ever."

"This is some delusion of a fevered brain!" cried Pride, beginning to look very angry.

"No, my fever has passed away, and with it all my vain delusions. To think myself superior to all others was a delusion; to think that Pride would make me happy was a delusion: to think that a wellfurnished head could make up for a haughty and selfish heart, that was the worst delusion of all!"

Pride still lingered, unwilling to depart, or to give up one whom he had so long regarded as his slave; but the sound of footsteps was now heard, and Lubin and Nelly appeared at the door. The little girl cast an uneasy, frightened glance at Pride, who scowled darkly on her in return. But Duty and Affection, the beautiful sisters, were accompanying the children to their home, and Pride, bold as he was, shrank back abashed at their calm, majestic presence.

Dick, though languid and weak, nerved himself now for a great and painful effort. He had never been accustomed to own himself wrong, and the thought of doing so, not privately but openly, in the presence of so many witnesses, brought the warm blood to his pallid cheek, and made his heart throb with excitement. But he knew no better way of proving to Pride that his empire indeed was over; no better way of making amends to Nelly for past unkindness and scorn. Raising himself, therefore, and supporting his weak frame by grasping the table beside him, he uttered these words, in a clear and distinct, though somewhat tremulous tone:"Nelly, before all, I ask your forgiveness for past unkind and foolish conduct, and thank you for the tender care which I have so little deserved; and I also ask Lubin's pardon"here Dick turned towards his brother"for having often provoked him by rude and mocking words."

Nelly's only reply was running forward and throwing her arms around Dick; Lubin warmly grasped his hand; Pride, grinding his teeth with suppressed fury, glared for a moment at the three, then, turning round with something like a yell, rushed away from the spot. Let us hope that he never returned!

"Well done, nobly done, brave boy!" exclaimed Duty, coming forward, the red rays of the setting sun streaming upon her glorious figure, and her face, which was bright with loveliness exceeding all mortal beauty. It was the first time that the wounded boy had ever received her praise; and how sweet fell its accents from her lips, those lips that falsehood never had stained!

"We were coming to see you," said gentle Affection, "and met these our young friends on the way."

"Coming to see me!" cried the invalid; "poor, helpless, ruined sufferer that I am!"

"Nay," said Affection, with a beaming smile, "speak not so gloomily of your state. I bring you the refreshing draught of Hope, to revive your spirits and restore your strength!"

As Affection spoke she poured out from a phial into a glass a sparkling effervescing liquid. Dick took it eagerly from her hand, and as he drank it as if drinking in life, Affection continued thus to address him:"You will soon recover from the effects of your accident, and be able with new vigour and energy to refurnish your own little cottage. You will easily make up for lost time; indeed, the loss which you have sustained is not so great as has been represented. Look with a hopeful eye on the future, with a thankful eye on the past; he cannot be very ignorant who is instructed by Duty, nor very poor who has at his command all the treasures of Affection!"

Back to contents

CHAPTER XXVIII.

EXPECTATION.

VERY bright and beautiful was the day on which Dame Desley returned to her family. The sun rose in the morning in full glory, all surrounded with rosy clouds. The breath of the air was soft and sweet as that of balmy Spring, and Autumn could only be known by the splendid mantle of yellow, red, and brown, which she had thrown over the trees and bushes. Even brook Bother itself seemed to sparkle and dance in the sunbeams, and the white houses of Education reflected the cheerful light.

Nelly rose early, her heart bounding with delight, and made everything ready in her cottage to welcome the mother whom she loved. As she was busily rubbing up some of her furniturefacts till they shone as brightly as mirrors, poor Lubin joined his sister, looking disconsolate and dull.

"Nelly," said he, rubbing his forehead, "I'm afraid that my cottage is not well furnished. I've no table, and scarcely a chair, my carpet is all in a muddle, and I'm afraid that my dear mother will be disappointedeven disgusted."

Nelly did not know what to reply, so she only shook her head gravely.

"Do you think, Nelly, that I'd have time to rush off to Education this morning and bring back a table, bed, and a couple of chairs on my back?"

Though Nelly was really sorry for her brother, she could hardly help smiling at the idea of fat little Lubin puffing, panting, and blowing, under such a formidable burden. "I fear that you have no time today," she replied, "for even one journey to the town of Education. We expect our dear mother early, and we all, except poor Dick, who is not strong enough yet, are going to meet her on the road."

Lubin rubbed his forehead harder than before. "Had it not been for that thief Procrastination!" he exclaimed,

"And Amusement Bazaar," suggested Nelly.

"Oh," exclaimed Lubin, half ready to cry, "what a stupid donkey I have been!"

"I wish," said the pitying Nelly, "that we were allowed to help each other more. Not that I have much furniture to spare, but how gladly would I give of that little!"

"That's impossible," sighed poor Lubin; "and even if you could stuff my empty cottage with a dozen or so of your facts, that would not hide the horrible DUNCE which Mr. Learning scrawled on my wall. To think of mother's seeing it! ugh! how dreadfully shocked she will be!" and Lubin gave his forehead an actual bang, as if to punish it for his own neglect.

"Well, Lubin dear," said Nelly in a soothing tone, "we may regret the mistakes of the past, but let them only make us more anxious to do more with our future hours. You will begin to work hard tomorrow, and carry away a good store from Arithmetic or General Knowledge."

"I believe the first thing that I should do," observed the rueful boy, "is to master that ladder of Spelling."

"True, you will never get on without that," said Nelly. "I daresay with patience and pains you will get a wellfurnished house after all."

Poor Lubin looked only half comforted; but hearing a slow, feeble step, he hastened with Nelly to support Dick, and lead him to his comfortable armchair.

"So mother is coming today, and you are all going to meet her," said the pale boy, with a languid smile.

"You will wait and welcome her here, dear brother," said Nelly.

"No," replied Dick, with quiet sadness; "I will await her in my own poor cottage, it is there that she expects to see me. Will you kindly support me thither? I have just enough strength to cross the sward."

"But" began Lubin, and stopped short.

"Why should you go there," said Nelly, "when you are so welcome to remain where you are? and"

"I know what you are thinking," observed Dick; "you think that I will not be able to bear looking on the change and the ruin. But it is better, Nelly, that I should see all. I have needed the bitter lesson. I would rather go thither at once, and accustom myself to the sight before my dear mother arrives."

As the boy was evidently in earnest, Lubin and Nelly made no further objections. Dick, supported by them on either side, soon crossed over to his cottage, and was placed in one of the chairs which had been brought out of his own little kitchen, that room having quite escaped the effects of the fire. Dick looked sadly but calmly around him.

"See," said Nelly, "matters are not so bad after all. The curtains are gone, and some of the facts, but the grate, fireirons, and fender are as good as ever, they only want a little rubbing up. A great part of the carpet is safe, and all your purchases from Grammar's Bazaar happened to be stowed in the kitchen, so you see that they have not suffered at all. When you get a little strength, dear Dick, you will soon make everything right; a few new purchases will render your cottage as beautiful as it was before the fire."

Dick smiled, and pressed the hand of his sister.

Matty now rushed in, all in a flutter. "I'm so glad that you have not started!" she exclaimed. "I could not have endured not to have been amongst the first to welcome my mother!"

"Go then, go all," said Dick.

"I do not like to leave you alone here," observed Nelly, lingering by the chair of her brother.

"I shall not be dull," replied Dick; "the bird Content is singing in your home, and I shall listen here to his strains. I should rather be alone for awhile; there is little chance now that my quiet will be disturbed either by Pride or Miss Folly."

So Lubin and his sisters departed, Dick remaining behind, rather thoughtful than sad. He was a changed boy from what he had been at the time when he had bounded over the brook, bearing the ladder of Spelling aloft; or when he had laughed at Lubin for his struggle with Alphabet, the strong little dwarf. Dick had become weak, so he could feel for weakness; an accident had swept away the best part of his wealth, so that he had a fellowfeeling for the poor. Dick had become more gentle, more humble, more kind; that which he had deemed a terrible misfortune, that which had laid him on a bed of sickness, had been in truth one of the happiest events of his life. He had gained much more than he had lost.

Dick sat for some time in eager expectation of his mother's arrival, listening to every noise, and keeping his watchful eye on the road which he could see through the open door. At last there was a sound as of advancing steps and eager voices; weak as he still was, Dick sprang to his feet, and in another minute, to his great delight, he was clasped to the heart of his mother.

CHAPTER XXIX.

EMPTY AND FURNISHED.

YOU find the poor cottage in a sad state," was Dick's melancholy observation, as his mother, after the first loving greeting, seated herself at his side, holding his thin hand in her own, and looking tenderly at his pale features.

"O mother, if you had only seen it before the fire!" exclaimed Nelly; "it was beautifulquite beautifulso much better furnished than any of ours!"

"It will be beautiful again," said Dame Desley, cheerfully; "my boy only wants a little more Timemoney when his strength is perfectly restored. And I can see," she added, rising and opening the backdoor, through which she could view the garden, "that great pains were once taken here."

"I have not been able to attend to it since my illness," said Dick; "but as soon as I am able to set to work again, I will try to get all into order."

"I must now go and examine the other cottages," said Dame Desley; "I noticed as I came here that the wall of Matty's had been scorched, and that the new thatch which has been put on does not look quite so well as the old; but I hear that the inside has sustained no harm, and I shall now examine with pleasure the furniture bought by my child."

As Dame Desley was proceeding to the next cottage, which, as we all know, was that of Lubin, whom should she meet but Mr. Learning, cane in hand, and spectacles on nose, with a white box under his arm.

"Oh, what on earth brings him here just now!" exclaimed Lubin to Nelly, ready to stamp with vexation; "as if it were not bad enough to have mother examining my poor empty cottage, without having him to look on all the time through those horrid spectacles, that will magnify every defect. Just hear now how mother is thanking him for all that he has done for her children, and see what a sly meaning glance he is casting at me, looking through his glasses, as much as to say'There's one stupid dunce of a fellow; I could never make anything of him.'"

"You will do better in future," whispered Nelly, as she went forward to shake hands with Mr. Learning, who benignantly smiled at his pupil.

"We will go in here first," said Dame Desley; "Lubin, dear, come to my side."

The poor boy would gladly have kept back, and had some thoughts of running away down the hill, so grievously was he ashamed that his mother and guardian should see what little use he had made of his hours. He dared not, however, disobey; so with Dame Desley on one side, and stately Mr. Learning on the other, feeling like a culprit between two constables, he entered his illfurnished cottage.

Dame Desley looked to the right hand, and then she looked to the left; and the longer she looked the longer grew her face, and the graver the expression which it wore. There was a terribly awkward silence. Nelly felt quite uncomfortable, and Lubin stood twisting the button on his jacket, and wishing himself up to the neck in brook Bother, or anywhere but at home. At last the mother spoke, but her accents were those of displeasure.

"What can you have done, stupid boy, with all your minutes and hours?"

"I gave some to my shopping" whimpered Lubin.

"Humph!" growled Mr. Learning.

"Very few, I fear," said Dame Desley.

"Procrastination picked my pocket of some, andand"

"I suspect that the frequenters of Amusement's Bazaar could tell us where the best part have gone," said Mr. Learning with freezing severity. "You have thrown away your minutes and your hours upon balls, ninepins, marbles, and lollypops."

What could poor Lubin reply? He knew that the accusation was too true. His distress reached its height on his seeing that the eyes of his mother were resting on the big dunce, which stared in black letters from the wall.

"Oh, that I could pummel Mr. Learning for writing it up there!" thought Lubin.

"I wonder that you do not blush to look at that!" exclaimed Dame Desley, in high displeasure. "This very day you must be off to Mr. Reading's, and get a respectable paper to cover that shameful wall."

"And don't forget the ladder of Spelling," cried Mr. Learning; "there's nothing to be done without that."

Nelly, who saw that Lubin's face was growing as red as the feathers of Parade, now timidly came forward to try and draw attention from the unhappy sluggard. "Dear mother, I hope that you remember that you have other cottages to see," she said, placing her hand in that of Dame Desley.

"And I hope that I shall find them very different indeed from this," said the disappointed parent, as she crossed over the way to Matty's.

The little owner ran on in front, with mingled feelings of hope and fear. She knew that her home was not empty; that the furniture looked very gay; but she could not help suspecting that her mother, and yet more the sage Mr. Learning, might think some of it tawdry and worthless. Flinging the door wide open to admit her guests, Matty ran in so hurriedly to put a piece of furniture straight, that her foot was caught in her unfastened carpet, and down she fell on her nose.

"My dear child, I hope that you're not hurt," cried Dame Desley.

Matty jumped up, rubbed her nose, and said that it was "nothing," though looking extremely annoyed at such a beginning to the survey.

"What a hole you have torn in the carpet!" cried her mother. "Why, it is not fastened down with nails; you must be in danger of tripping every minute."

"Such a carpet!" exclaimed Learning, with contempt, kicking it up with his heel.

"And what a paper!" cried the mother; "as shabby as it is gaudy, and all with the damp showing through."

"But I have some things very pretty indeed," said Matty, in rather a petulant tone; for she could not bear that any fault should be found with her beautiful cottage. "I'm sure that the porcelain jars on the mantelpiece are fit for the palace of a princess; and just look at my gilded French mirror, and my elegant tambourine."

Dame Desley appeared by no means as much delighted at these fine things as her daughter had expected; and Mr. Learning dryly observed, "I see that you have troubled Mr. Arithmetic, the ironmonger, as little as Mr. History, the carpet manufacturer; and however pretty your fancy articles may be, I must just venture to remark that a poker is more useful than porcelain, a mat than a gilded French mirror, and that, though a tambourine may be charming, it can't supply the place of a table."

"Your furniture also looks so light and fragile," observed Dame Desley, "that I should be almost afraid to use it."

"Oh, it does exceedingly well," cried the mortified Matty, tossing herself down on a chair, to show that her mother was mistaken. She had chosen, however, an unfortunate way of displaying the strength of her furniture; the luckless chair gave way with a crash, and Matty came down with a thumping blownot this time on her nose, but on the back of her head.

More hurt than she had been by her former tumble, and yet more mortified than hurt, the poor child began to cry. Dame Desley and Nelly ran to raise her, while Mr. Learning, grave as he usually was, could hardly refrain from laughing.

"She has quite a bump on her poor head!" cried Nelly. "Dear Matty! what can we do for her?"

"Get me the pink salve from the mantelpiece," sobbed Matty. Her sister hurried to the place as fast as she could.

"Let me see it first," said Dame Desley, examining the little china pot, which was labelled, "Flattery Salve, patronized by the nobility and gentry. Warranted to heal all manner of bruises and sores."

"Where did you get this?" inquired the mother. Matty whimpered out that she had had it from Miss Folly.

"Let Miss Folly keep her own trash to herself!" cried the indignant dame, flinging the little pot out of the window; "that is a most dangerous salve: its effect is often that of injuring the brain, weakening the sensesproducing dizziness and delirium! Bring a little cold water, Nelly; that is a far better thing to apply to a bump on the head like this."

"I am afraid," observed Mr. Learning, as the simple remedy was tried with effect, "that Matty, quick and ready a pupil as she is, will have almost as much to do as Lubin before her cottage is really well furnished. She had better at once commence the work of getting rid of the trash; and I should recommend her to make a famous large bonfire of it to celebrate her mother's return."

Poor Matty, who had at first eyed with mingled curiosity and hope the white box under the arm of her guardianbelieving that it must contain the silver crown of Successfelt her heart sink at these words; and with drooping head and melancholy mien, she went with her companions to the cottage adjoining.

CHAPTER XXX.

FRUITS OF NEEDLEWORK.

NOW this is what I should call neatneat, and not gaudy," said Dame Desley, as she stood in the doorway of Nelly's home, and surveyed with a pleased eye the perfect order of the place. "The fireirons bright, though smallthe paper chosen with judgmenteverything needful, though there is little to spareeach article in its proper place, and neat and good of its kind." Oh, how delightful to Nelly was the praise which she had fairly earned by selfdenying labour!

"Considering that Nelly is lamethat she has never been gifted either with quickness or strength, I have every reason," observed Mr. Learning, "to be satisfied with what she has done."

"And what a beautiful bird; and how tame!" cried Dame Desley, as Content, recognizing a friend, hopped lightly down to her finger.

"That was the gift of my dear friend, Duty," said Nelly.

"A friend whom you cannot prize too much, or follow too closely," observed her mother.

"Here she comes herself!" cried Nelly in joyful surprise, "and sweet Affection behind her! They have doubtless come here today to welcome home my dear mother."

The meeting was a very joyous one. Duty and Affection had for many years been the valued friends of Dame Desley.

After the first words of greeting had passed between them, Affection inquired whether the dame had seen the gardens of her daughters, and looked at their needlework plants.

"Not yet, but I am going to examine them," replied the mother.

"Let us all come together!" said Duty.

With a very low bow of respect, Mr. Learning offered his arm to the noble maiden; Affection rested one hand on Dame Desley's, and, smiling, held out the other to Nelly; Lubin and Matty followed behindthe boy somewhat sulky and sad, but the girl with reviving spirits. Matty was a little jealous of the praises which her sister had received; but she expected in the garden, if not in the cottage, to be found far superior to poor, lame Nelly.

The gardens of Nelly and Matty were divided from each other only by a boxhedge, which was scarcely three inches high. The party, though entering from Nelly's backdoor, went immediately into the garden of her sister, as Dame Desley thought that it was right to attend first to that of the elder.

Both gardens won a fair meed of praise. Matty, as has before been mentioned, happened to be fond of geographical flowers; and while the arrangement of the two gardens was equally neat and correct, Matty had certainly a larger number of countries and capitals to display.

"I should not wonder," whispered Matty to Lubin, "if I were to win the silver crown of Success after all."

Lubin's only answer was a sigh; for he knew that he had lost all chance of getting the prize.

"And now for the needlework plants," said Dame Desley, approaching the gardenwall.

Every one uttered an exclamation of pleasure on beholding Matty's beautiful creeper. Ripe fruits, with rosy down like that upon the peach, hung on its twining boughs, looking lovelier by contrast with its green and shining leaves. Matty plucked one, and offered it to her mother. The dame quickly removed the rind, and a delicate little beadpurse met her admiring gaze. It was of pink and gold, with tiny tassels to match. Matty pulled another fruit from the bough, and it offered to view a pretty beadmat, with a pattern of flowers upon it.

"Well, that is a fine plant!" observed Mr. Learning, admiration in his spectacled eyes.

Matty triumphantly squeezed Lubin's arm. "I think that I shall get the prize," she whispered. "I should have been sure of it if that stupid chair had not given me such an unfortunate tumble. How ugly Nelly's plant looks yonder, with its large, coarse, prickly stem; and it grows so close to the ground. I should be ashamed to have such a thing in my garden!"

"Now for Nelly's needlework," said Affection.

The whole party moved on to the spot, when they saw a plantnot beautiful, it must be owned, but with three fruits, as big as pumpkins, resting upon the ground, half covered with large green leaves.

"Shall I pluck one?" said Nelly, modestly.

"Let us see it," replied Mr. Learning.

Nelly stooped, and broke from its stalk the smallest of the fruits. It was so ripe that the rind burst open in her hands, and out dropped a cap as white as snow, with a number of delicate frills all neatly hemmed and gathered. With a smile and a blush, Nelly presented her little offering to her mother, while a murmur of approbation sounded from all around.

"Ah, how useful this will be!" exclaimed Dame Desley; "this fruit is charming indeed!"

"Let us see the others," said Duty, bending forward to gaze.

Again Nelly stooped and raised the ripe fruit; again it burst open in her grasp. She pulled out an apron, very prettily made, with neat little pockets in front!

"The very thing that I have been wanting!" cried the dame, putting it on with pleasure and pride.

"There's more yet to be seen," said Mr. Learning.

The third fruit was so very big, that but for the assistance of both Duty and Affection, Nelly would hardly have known how to manage. It was not quite so ripe as the others, and would not come readily from the thick stalk, and the rind did not burst open as those of the two first had done.

"How can we see what is in it?" cried Matty.

"Something very good is in it, no doubt," said Affection; and Duty, pulling a pair of scissors out of her pocket, soon decided the question. A great hole was made in the rind, and all the party pressed round with curiosity to watch the little girl, who now began slowly to draw out the gray contents of the fruit.

"I say," exclaimed Lubin, "what's that long thing?it looks for all the world like a sleeve."

"The body is coming after," cried Matty.

Yes, sure enough it was coming, body and skirt and alla nice, new, warm dress, for Dame Desley to wear through the approaching winter.

When the whole of the huge fruit was emptied, and the gown held up by Affection, there was a general clapping of hands, in admiration of the wonderful plant. Matty alone looked coldly upon it, and observed in a low tone to Lubin, that such a dress as that would certainly never be worn by Lady Fashion.

"Nor made by her most particular friend," laughed Lubin, who had half forgotten his own troubles in Nelly's triumph. "Depend upon it that a sensible dress like that was never stitched by Miss Folly."

"We may congratulate Nelly," said Duty, "upon the success of her Plainwork. I wish that every girl in the land had such a plant in her garden."

"I think that none of us can doubt," observed Mr. Learning, taking the white box from under his arm, "which of our four young friends has made the best use of Timemoneywhich has best deserved the crown of Success." And opening the box, he took out a most elegant wreath of leaves worked in filigree silver, and made an attempt to place it on the head of the blushing Nelly. But the little girl modestly shrank back.

"Oh, no!" cried Nelly; "it is not for me. It would not be right, it would not be fair, that poor Dick should lose what he had fairly earned, because Folly set his furniture on fire. Lubin can witness, Matty can witness, that his cottage was far better furnished than mine before the accident happened. Indeed the crown ought to be his. I could not bear to deprive him of it."

Duty smiled kindly at the little pleader; Affection stooped down and gave her a kiss.

"I must say," observed honest Lubin, in answer to Nelly's appeal, "that none of us cut such a dash as Dick did before that unlucky explosion."

"Nelly," said Mr. Learning, with a most benevolent air, "the crown is yoursI give it to you. You may bear it to your brother, if you will."

The lame girl waited for no further permission, but hurried off at the greatest speed which she could command, to carry to another the prize which she herself might have worn.

"After all, I believe that Nelly has deserved all the praise and love which she has won," sighed the disappointed Matty, her jealousy conquered by the example of generous selfdenial which she saw in her younger sister.

The party quickly followed the steps of Nelly Desley to the cottage of DickLubin assisting his mother to carry the various gifts of his sisters. Affection quitted the rest for a few minutes in order to direct the movements of some attendants, who were spreading a table in the open air, in the space between the cottages. They were making preparations for a banquet, designed as a pleasant surprise for the Desleys upon their mother's return. The treat was given by Duty and Affection upon the joyful occasion, and especially intended to honour the wearer of the crown of Success.

Back to contents

CHAPTER XXXI.

THE CROWN OF SUCCESS.

MINE, Nelly! no, it can never be mine!" exclaimed Dick, resisting with emotion the efforts of his sister to place the crown on his head.

"It was to be for the one who had made the best use of his hours," said Nelly; "it is fairly yours, for none of our furniture could be compared to that which you brought from the town. It was not your fault that an accident destroyed what had cost you so many good hours, nor is it right that you should suffer a double loss from the fire."

"There might have been reason in what you say," observed the pale invalid, "if the accident had indeed been owing to no error of my own. Nay, Nelly, you must not prevent me from telling the whole truth. It is best that I should speak, and that all these my friends should hear." Dame Desley, her children, and her guests, were all standing around the boy. "If," continued Dick, "I had obeyed the voice of my motherif I had turned my back upon Pride, and not attempted, at his bidding, things that I was not able to performif he had not introduced me to Folly, whom I encouraged, although I despised herthe explosion would never have taken place, I should have suffered no shame and loss. I am willing to bear the consequences of my own wilfulness and presumption. I should blush to wear the crown of Success, which I feel that I do not merit. Let me see it on your brow, dear Nelly; its proper place is there. Next to the pleasure of winning it myself, is that of knowing that it belongs to one who so richly deserves it."

Nelly was no longer able to resist. The sparkling crown was placed on her brow. Lubin congratulated her with frank kindness, and even Matty felt that she had no right to complain. The reflection, however, passed through the mind of the girl, "All this honour and pleasure might have been mine, had I never listened to Folly!"

And now Mr. Learning came forward, and stood in the centre of the circle, leaning one hand on the armchair of Dick, while with the other he motioned for silence. It was clear, from his preparatory cough, that the sage was going to make a speech.

"My friends," he began, in his distinct, solemn tone, glancing benignly around, "we are all met together on a happy occasion. We see merit rewarded with success, and patient obedience to Duty achieving more than talent or genius. Before we proceed to the banquet to which our fair friends have invited us, let me mention before all my intentions in regard to the future year. When twelve months have run their course I will again return to this place, again look for a kindly welcome, again examine the cottages here. If I find that Dick has made up for the pastthat Matty, giving up all connection with Folly, has furnished wisely and wellthat Lubin, by steady perseverance, has made all forget that the word DUNCE was ever inscribed on his wallnot only one, but all and each of my young friends shall receive a crown of Success."

"Hurrah! hurrah!" shouted Lubin, who had just been forming a number of good resolutions. A smile of pleasure lit up the pale features of Dick; and Matty, in expectation, already felt the silver crown on her head.

"And now," said graceful Duty, "let Mr. Learning conduct our Nelly to the feast prepared, as she is Queen of the day."

Even Dick, as if gaining fresh strength from the sight of the pleasant company around him, was able, leaning on his mother, to join the cheerful circle that on that beautiful autumnal day gathered around the board. Conversation flowed freely, nothing painful was recalled, no one whispered about Pride, no one mentioned Miss Folly. Brightly sparkled the beverage of Hope, foaming and bubbling in the glass; and every one who has tasted it knows what a delicious beverage it is. The stores of Amusement had been half emptied to furnish sweetmeats and cakes for the table; and Affection had provided a large quantity of the dried fruits of sweet Recollections. Merry were the smiles that were exchanged; merry the jests that were made; merriest of all the loud song of Content, as he warbled his lay of delight, fluttering round the head of her who wore the silver crown of Success.

And I now would gather around me my readers, to make them a little address ere we part. I see them in my mind's eyefrom the schoolboy with jacket and cap, who has thought it a condescension to read such "childish stuff," to the little curlyheaded urchin in tartan frock, who, when taking a drive with mamma, asks whether the little stream which he passes be not "the real brook Bother." There is the tall elder sister, who only reads aloud "to amuse the children;" and the girl who "hates all lessons;" and the little laughing fairy who expects some day to see dwarf Alphabet standing at the door of a shop. It is not hard to make a speech when no one can see the speaker. So, without blushing, or coughing, or stammering, A. L. O. E. addresses her readers.

Have not you, my friends, been reading in my story of persons and scenes with which you yourselves are familiar? Have you not each a nice little head to furnish, and Timemoney to pay for your purchases? And do not all your best friends recommend you to go to the good town of Education? Do not you know the muddy brook Bother? Have you not crossed it on the plank of Patience; or have you neverpray pardon the questiongone floundering right into the middle? I am pretty sure that you have paid toll to Alphabet, the stout little dwarf; that you have felt how troublesome and tedious it is to climb Multiplication staircase; that you have examined Reading's fine shop; glanced at

Arithmetic's grates and fireirons; and probably tumbled many a time from that awkward ladder of Spelling. Have I not amongst my young audience a clever Dick, a lazy Lubin, a silly Matty, and a lame little child like Nelly? Each reader must judge for himself which character most resembles his own, and let each kindly accept a suitable word of advice.

Clever reader! beware of Pride. Don't let him lurk behind your doordon't let him lead you to cut either your fingers or your friends, by attempting things for which you are not fitted, or by looking down upon companions not gifted with powers like your own. Do not despise Patience, or think that you are too clever to need it. It is not the quickest or sharpest pupil that really spends Time to best purpose. Often has the haughty, selfwilled genius been found to forfeit the crown of Success.

Lazy reader! you who love play far better than work, and are tempted to vote Education, its tradesmen, its family of Ologies, and all, as the greatest bores in the world, beware of Procrastinationbeware of the thief of Timebeware of putting off till tomorrow what ought to be done today. Can you bear to see that word dunce so terribly distinct on your wall? Can you bear to throw away on nothing but Amusement those precious hours and minutes which, well employed, might gain for you the silver crown of Success?

Silly reader!but here I must pause, for it is probable that no little girl glancing over my pages will accept the title as her own. Yet, if she know Miss Folly, delight in her gossiping prate, dress according to her fanciful taste, and value her poisonous salve, she must really excuse me for classing her with our poor, conceited young Matty. There are thousands and tens of thousands, I fear, of such silly girls in the world (some of them may possibly be amongst my readers), who would furnish their heads with bubbles, and neglect the good for the gay. To such I would utter a gentle warning. Folly can never lead you to real happiness or real usefulness in the world. She may promise you pleasures for a moment; but her pleasures either vanish into air, or leave pain and vexation behind. Then shut her out from your home; give her idle fancies no room. Let your dress be sober, neat, and quietsuited to the station in which you are placed. Girls who deck themselves out to be admired remind us of the cockatoo Parade, puffing out its red feathers, and always repeating the cry, "Ain't I fine? ain't I fine?" Let your furniture be useful and solid; water well the plant of Plainwork. It is not the fanciful, frivolous miss who merits the crown of Success.

But, perhaps, amongst my audience are several who may be described as lame, from the difficulty with which they make their way to the town of Education. They can hardly climb up hill Puzzle, and are often tempted to sit down in despair by the swollen waters of Bother! Courage, my dear young friends! Resolute perseverance will yet win the crown of Success. If you keep your eye upon Duty, and bravely follow where she would leadif, guided by gentle Affection, you steadily pursue a right courseyou will conquer difficulties at last, be useful, honoured, and beloved.

But if you would further know how to find out Duty, and, having found her, how to get strength and courage to follow her precepts, remember, dear friends, what was the best gift that even Affection could offer. There is something better than human knowledgesomething stronger than mortal effortssomething more precious than earthly Success! Oh, make it your own, for only when that is possessed will the bird Content fold its silver wings, and rest in your bosoms for ever!

Back to contents

The "Little Hazel" Series.

EIGHT VOLUMES BY THE AUTHOR OF "LITTLE HAZEL."

Post vo, cloth extra. Price s. d. each.

Little Frida; or, The King's Messenger. By the Author of "Little Hazel, the King's Messenger," etc.

The story of a little girl who was found by a woodcutter in the Black Forest in Germany, and was taken to his home and brought up there by his kindhearted wife along with her own children.

The Crown of Glory; or, "Faithful unto Death." A Scottish Story of Martyr Times. By the Author of "Little Hazel, the King's Messenger."

A tale, founded on history, regarding the first medical missionary in Scotland.

The Guiding Pillar. A Story for the Young. By the Author of "Under the Old Oaks; or, Won by Love."

An interesting tale for the young, illustrating the sure guidance of the pillarcloud of Providence for all willing to follow in humble faith.

Little Hazel, the King's Messenger. By the Author of "Little Snowdrop and Her Golden Casket," etc.

A story for the young, showing what a Christian child may do.

Little Snowdrop and Her Golden Casket. By the Author of "Little Hazel, the King's Messenger," etc.

A tale for the young, illustrative of the preciousness of Scripture promises.

The Royal Banner; or, Gold and Rubies. A Story for the Young. By the Author of "Little Snowdrop and Her Golden Casket," etc.

A wellwritten story of home and school life. Cannot fail to prove interesting.

"Thy Kingdom Come." A Tale for Boys and Girls.

Under the Old Oaks; or, Won by Love. By the Author of "Little Hazel, the King's Messenger," etc.

UNIFORM WITH "LITTLE HAZEL" SERIES.

Little Tora, the Swedish Schoolmistress; And Other Stories. By Mrs. Woods Baker, Author of "The Swedish Twins," etc.

"Charming idyllic pictures of Swedish life."Scotsman.

A Helping Hand. By M. B. Synge, Author of "A Child of the Mews," etc.

Archie's Chances. By the Author of "The Spanish Brothers," etc. With Illustrations.

Alive in the Jungle. A Story for the Young. By Eleanor Stredder, Author of "Jack and His Ostrich," etc.

A fascinating story of childsnatching by a wolf, of the life led by the child in the wolf's lair, and of the cunning device of a native hunter to effect the rescue of the child.

Milton Keynes UK
Ingram Content Group UK Ltd.
UKHW010703260923
429409UK00004B/380